Harry Turner Newcomb

Railway Economics

Harry Turner Newcomb

Railway Economics

ISBN/EAN: 9783742810748

Manufactured in Europe, USA, Canada, Australia, Japa

Cover: Foto ©Andreas Hilbeck / pixelio.de

Manufactured and distributed by brebook publishing software
(www.brebook.com)

Harry Turner Newcomb

Railway Economics

BY

H. T. NEWCOMB, LL. M.

Chief of the Section of Freight Rates in the Division of Statistics of the
United States Department of Agriculture and
Instructor in Statistics and Transportation in Columbian University.

PHILADELPHIA :
RAILWAY WORLD PUBLISHING CO.
1898.

PRESS OF
PATTERSON & WHITE, PHILA.

PREFACE.

THIS little work, originally prepared for serial publication in the RAILWAY WORLD, was intended to
present the principal facts which establish the
position of railway transportation in the present organization of industry in the United States, with only so
much of comment and discussion as seemed absolutely
necessary in order to define the relations among those
facts. The present publication is due to the belief that
while more extended treatment of some of the subjects
than is here given is unquestionably desirable, a concise
and untechnical statement may, in view of the necessities of the present situation, prove more generally serviceable than a larger and more ambitious work.

H. T. N.

U. S. Department of Agriculture.
WASHINGTON, October, 1898.

CONTENTS.

Railway Economics.

CHAPTER I.

TRANSPORTATION.

Beginning approximately with the last quarter of the eighteenth century and continuing throughout that just closing there has been an almost revolutionary change in the organization and methods of productive industry. Among the most characteristic features of this change is the increased importance of the transportation element in production. At the commencement of the period the necessary articles of subsistence were, with few exceptions, wholly produced within the localities in which they were required for consumption, and exchanges between distant communities were practically restricted to articles of great value used only by those able to indulge in expensive luxuries. Means of transportation by water had improved but little, and those for transportation by land scarcely at all since the dawn of history. The movement of commodities was so costly as to be prohibitive of exchanges of ordinary food or textile products, so slow that perishable articles could traverse but the shortest distances, and accompanied by such excessive risks that at a few hundred miles from the regions of production the prices of even the most costly articles were doubled, trebled, or quadrupled. The contrast offered at the present time is extreme.

The world is traversed by almost innumerable lines of transportation; there is scarcely a habitable region, however small or scantily peopled, that is not regularly served by railways or steamships, and nearly every community, no matter how backward in civilization and culture, depends upon exchanging some surplus product with other communities for necessary articles of ordinary and constant use. Nations, no longer economically independent, are classified as manufacturing or agricultural in accordance with the character of the surplus products with which they enter the world's markets. Especially in the United States the differentiation and localization of industry have gone very far, and to furnish the more luxurious articles of clothing and food for the citizens of this country commodities are brought from all points of the globe. The wage-earner in New York city wears clothing made of woolens manufactured in Massachusetts from wool grown in Montana, mixed, too often, with cotton grown in Texas. He drinks coffee from Brazil, Central America or Mexico, and tea from China or Japan, sweetened with sugar from Germany, the Eastern or Western Indies, or Louisiana, and mixed, perhaps, with milk brought two hundred miles from the interior of the state. His bread is made from flour ground in Minneapolis from wheat grown in the Dakotas. He eats beef raised in Texas and killed in Chicago, bacon cured in Kansas City, Omaha, or St. Louis, and, not infrequently, eggs laid in Iowa; oranges and lemons from Bermuda or the shores of the Mediterranean, raisins and preserved fruits from Spain or California, figs and dates from Italy, and spices from India are not too expensive for his table; the holiday finery worn by his wife is adorned with the products of France, and toys made in Germany amuse his children.

The marine engine and the locomotive have been the principal instruments in effecting this change, of which merchant fleets and railway trains constitute, to many at least, the most tangible expression. The significance of the change is this: Differences in soil and climate, in mineral resources, in the character and capacity of workmen, render particular regions peculiarly adaptable to certain forms of production. A region of sterile soil which responds grudgingly and meagerly to the arts of the husbandman may abound in mineral wealth or be plentifully supplied with water power. Without modern transportation facilities the latter must remain undeveloped, or subsistence for those engaged in exploiting them must be obtained in spite of disadvantages and difficulties from the former. In any event, the mineral or water power could not be completely utilized, for the distribution of the products of either would be confined within a narrow area and a considerable portion of the aggregate energy of the community would necessarily be devoted to the cultivation of the soil. Under modern conditions the entire available energy of the community would be devoted to the exploitation of the mines or water power and the surplus production, distributed widely wherever needed, would purchase those articles of necessity and luxury which could be produced by the community itself, if at all, only with an unnecessary and wasteful expenditure of effort. It is evident therefore that by permitting the specialization of industrial functions and making possible a territorial

division of labor under which only that share in producing the complex of articles necessary for the satisfaction of the wants of society at large for which it is
best adapted is assigned to each locality, the development of transportation facilities has multiplied the productive efficiency of both capital and labor.

The transportation element had such an insignificant
relation to industry, as conducted a century ago, that
it is scarcely too much to say that its development has
added a new form of production. A quantity of wheat
in excess of that demanded by the local-population has
in North Dakota no value save that which is due to the
fact that it can be transported and utilized to feed the
inhabitants of distant and less fertile regions; yet it represents an expenditure of productive energy and has
gained a part of the total capacity for satisfying desires
that it will possess when in the hands of actual consumers. This capacity for satisfying desires which will
be at its maximum when, transformed into bread, the
wheat is in the possession of those who are to consume
it, constitutes its utility and is found, on analysis, to have
been produced by a series of acts which can be classified
as having given it, respectively, form and position.
Those who tilled the soil called into operation natural
forces which, taking a certain amount of carbon from
the atmosphere and of hydrogen, oxygen and nitrogen
from the soil, endowed them with the form utility of
wheat; it was moved by rail to Minneapolis, and having
been placed where it could be made into flour, gained a
place utility, to which the millers added a utility of form.
The railway from Minneapolis to the point of consumption contributed an additional utility of place; the baker

making it into bread and distributing the product, gave both form and place utilities. Nearly all commodities of current use represent the combined productive efforts of those who create, respectively, form utilities and place utilities. The effect of the development of modern transportation agencies has been to give relatively greater importance to the production of place utilities.

Railway transportation is commonly regarded as cheap transportation, and if the aggregate cost of the transportation performed by railways is compared with the number of units moved, the average obtained is very low; but, on the other hand, so great a portion of the aggregate productive energy of society as at present was never at any other period devoted to transportation. Every successive decrease in the average cost per unit of service has so increased the demand for transportation and has constituted such an impetus to territorial exchanges that it has augmented rather than reduced the total expenditure for transportation. The economic interests of society demand that the satisfaction of human wants be secured with the least practicable expenditure of energy, not that either form utilities in particular or place utilities in particular be produced more cheaply. The real gain from the change in transportation methods has been that it has reduced the total social cost of subsistence by permitting form utilities to be given to each commodity under the most favorable conditions which can be discovered.

CHAPTER II.

RAILWAY SERVICE IN THE UNITED STATES.

Because of the wide area of the United States, the diverse natural resources of the country, and the extent in which the localization of industry has been permitted by unrestricted domestic trade, facilities for cheap, rapid and safe transportation constitute a most important element in their economic organization. Though there are within the United States lakes vast enough to float the commerce of the world and mighty rivers unequaled elsewhere within the domain of civilization, these natural waterways are but auxiliaries to the general system of transportation, which partly on account of the topography of the country and the normal trend of commercial shipments is mainly overland. The early contest for supremacy between canals and railways demonstrated the comparative inadequacy of the former for any service other than that of feeders for the more efficient system. The railways speedily gained and have successfully maintained a paramount position in the national transportation system.

During the seven decades that comprehend the period of steam railway transportation there have been constructed throughout the world 445,000 miles of railway, which are capitalized at about $35,000,000,000. Though the United States occupy approximately but six per cent. of the land surface of the earth and contain an even smaller proportion of its total population, they are traversed by 41 per cent. of this mileage, represented by 30 per cent. of the capital. The aggregate length of the railways of the United States on June 30, 1897, was 184,428 miles, or six times as great as in any other country, and exceeded the length of the lines serving the whole of Europe by 25,000 miles.

It is not sufficient to measure the transportation facilities of a nation in miles; the true criterion is their relation to the demand for the movement of persons and property. Exact determination of the extent of this demand is practically impossible, but approximately accurate conclusions can be reached by comparing mileage with population and area. So measured, the people of the United States are served by a greater length of railways in proportion to their number than those of any other country except Orange Free State and some of the provinces of Australasia. For every 10,000 of inhabitants the United States have 26.0 miles of railway; Great Britian and Ireland, 5.2; Germany, 5.6; France, 6.6; Russia, including Finland, 2.2; Spain, 4.2; Brazil, 4.7; Argentina, 19.6; British North America, 22.4; and Australasia, 31.6. The proportion of railway mileage to area is exceeded only in the most densely populated countries of Europe. With 6.1 miles of railway for every 100 square miles of land area, the United States are surpassed by Great Britian and Ireland with 17.4; by Belgium with 31.4; by the Netherlands and Luxemburg with 14.0; by Germany with 14.0; by Switzerland with 13.8; by France with 12.2; by Italy with 8.5; by Denmark with 9.3; and by Austria-Hungary, including Bosnia, with 7.6. The average for the whole of Europe is but 4.2 miles; for Brazil, 0.2; for Argentina, 0.6; for British North America, 0.3; and for Australasia, 0.3.

The number of passengers annually carried by the

railways of the United States is exceeded in but one country, England; it is twice as great as in France, and more than 50 per cent. greater than in the German Empire. The freight tonnage annually carried by the railways in this country is greater than the totals for Great Britain and Ireland, France, and Germany combined, and the average distance traversed is much longer.

The following statement shows the number of miles of railroad in the United States, at each census year, the increase during each decade, and the relation of mileage to population and area at each date:

Years.	Length in miles.	Increase in miles.	Increase, per cent.	Number of miles per—	
				10,000 of population.	100 square miles of area.
1830	40	......	.....	0.03	....
1840	2,755	2,715	6,788	1.61	0.13
1850	8,571	5,816	211	3.71	0.29
1860	28,920	20,348	237	9.20	0.97
1870	49,168	20,249	70	12.75	1.66
1880	87,724	38,556	78	17.49	2.95
1890	163,562	75,838	86	26.12	5.51

More than half of the present railway mileage has been constructed since 1880. Of this increase 56 per cent. is in the states and territories west of the Mississippi, where it is equal to 184 per cent. of the mileage of 1880; 19½ per cent. is east of the Mississippi, and south of the Ohio and Potomac, where the increase is 115 per cent. of the mileage previously constructed in that section; and 25 per cent. is in the region east of the Mississippi and north of the Ohio and the Potomac, where the mileage constructed since 1880 is 53 per cent. of what then existed in that section. The evident conclusion is that in some of the older portions of the country the railway system is now practically completed; and this is

confirmed by the very small percentages of increase during the last two decades in most of the New England
States.

The following table shows the railway mileage of the
country on June 30 of each year from 1880 to 1897,
inclusive, with the annual increase. The figures given
for operated mileage include a duplication of physical
mileage to the extent of from 3000 to 5000 miles owing
to the use of the same tracks by two or more companies.
Both physical and operated mileage are shown for those
years for which such complete data are available, the
figures being all from official sources:

Year.	Physical mileage.	Operated mileage, includ- ing trackage rights.	Annual increase.
1880	87,801.00	89,762.68	......
1881	....	97,868.19	8,105.51
1882	....	108,983.70	11,115.51
1883	....	118,734.54	9,750.84
1884	....	124,303.09	5,558.55
1885	....	127,099.42	2,796.33
1886	....	133,369.40	6,269.98
1887	....	145,409.91	12,040.51
1888	149,901.72	154,730.06	9,320.15
1889	157,758.83	160,835.58	7,857.11
1890	163,597.05	166,841.64	5,838.22
1891	168,402.74	172,221.25	4,805.69
1892	171,563.52	175,509.35	3,160.78
1893	176,461.07	180,581.27	4,897.55
1894	178,708.55	182,894.37	2,247.48
1895	180,657.47	184,944.44	1,948.92
1896	182,776.63	187,003.74	2,119.16
1897	184,428.47	....	1,651.84

The table shows two periods of heavy railway construction since 1880, culminating in 1882 and 1887,
each followed by a gradual falling off in the amount of
new line built. The annual increase in operated mileage
cannot be taken to represent exactly the amount of new
construction, but if both figures could be given they

would not be far apart. Using round numbers, therefore, it may be said that the amount of new line annually constructed has fluctuated between 12,000 miles in 1886-87, and less than 1700 miles in 1896-97. The average annual increase during the period covered by the table was 5684 miles, but for the last five years it was only 2573 miles. It should be understood that these figures represent miles of line, not miles of track. The inclusion of second, third, and fourth tracks, yard tracks, and sidings would swell the present total to nearly 245,000 miles. The equipment of the railways on June 30, 1897, included 35,986 locomotives, of which 10,017 were devoted to passenger, 20,398 to freight, and 5102 to switching service; the balance being unclassified. There were also 33,626 passenger cars, 1,221,730 freight cars, and 42,124 cars in company's service. As these data do not include equipment owned otherwise than by railway corporations, the number of freight cars is probably considerably understated.

The operation of the railway system required the service of 823,476 men during 1897, or about one in every thirty persons in the entire country engaged in gainful pursuits, and they received in wages and salaries $465,-601,581, or 62 per cent. of the entire expenditure of the railways for operation. These figures by no means adequately represent the labor incident to the operation and maintenance of the railway system. Statistics upon this subject in order to be complete would have to include those engaged in constructing cars and locomotives, in mining coal for the latter, in getting out ore and turning it into rails, and in a thousand other occupations seemingly independent of railway business.

CHAPTER III.

CAPITALIZATION.

American ingenuity has provided the railway facilities of the United States at a lower average cost per mile than in any other country in which due regard is paid to the requirements of speed and safety. The average capitalization of the railways of this country amounts to less than $60,000 per mile, and this includes such costly special construction as the sunken tracks of the New York Central and Hudson River Railroad in New York city; the tunnel that carries the Baltimore and Ohio Railroad underneath the city of Baltimore, and that which pierces the Hoosac Mountain for the Fitchburg Railroad; the elaborate block-signal systems of the Pennsylvania Railroad and other companies; the triumphs of engineering skill required to carry the Denver and Rio Grande Railroad and other Pacific lines over the Rocky Mountains; the numerous expensive bridges crossing the Mississippi, the Missouri, the Ohio, and other rivers; and many other extraordinary expenditures rendered essential by the development of the standard by which the adequacy of a modern transportation system is measured. Yet in spite of the high standard established by American demands in regard to the quality of service the average capitalization per mile in this country is little more than one-quarter of that in England, less than half that in France and Belgium and not more than two-thirds of that of Germany, Austria-Hungary, and Switzerland. The quality of service in Holland, Denmark, Norway, Sweden and Bul-

garia—the only European countries having a lower
average capitalization than the United States—is not
high enough to invalidate the conclusion. On the latest
dates for which data were available railway capital in
the United States averaged $156.23 *per capita* and $3901
per square mile of land surface. For Great Britain and
Ireland the corresponding figures were $124.49 and
$40,111, respectively; for France $84.45 and $15,635;
for Germany $53.34 and $13,131.

The total outstanding capitalization of the railways
of the United States on June 30, 1897, had a par value
of $10,635,008,074, of which $4,367,056,657 was common stock, $997,585,598 preferred stock, $4,539,911,595
mortgage bonds, $259,847,154 income bonds, $39,888,-
767 equipment trust obligations, and $430,718,303 mis-
cellaneous obligations. There were also outstanding
unfunded current liabilities amounting to $578,501,635.

A great deal of controversy not unmarked by angry
vehemence has centered about the relation of the present aggregate railway capitalization to the actual original cost of the properties which it represents. The opportunity for divergent opinion presented by this question is considerable. What is to be considered actual
cost? Is it to be defined as the amount paid for labor
and materials by those directly purchasing them; the
amount paid to a construction company, which may
have had to devise means for securing available funds
as well as to provide materials and labor; or is it to include the discounts necessary on bonds and stock before timid capital could be induced to undertake the
new enterprise? Some suggestions by Professor Henry
C. Adams in his first annual report as Statistician to the

Interstate Commerce Commission indicate a few of the difficulties.

"Is it, for example, possible to discover the cost and value of the carriers' property, franchises, and equipment? The papers giving evidence respecting these facts may have been destroyed, or in the fierce struggle of rival managements for control of territory by means of the absorption of lines already built the records of the original companies may have been lost, the consolidated companies caring nothing for records, except such as prove their right to the property absorbed. But of greater significance is the fact that in many instances the books of railway companies do not go beyond settlements with construction companies; that is to say, the investigation demanded by Congress is pushed back into the realm of vest-pocket book-keeping and a conveniently failing memory."

One fact which is almost invariably lost sight of in these discussions is that the construction of a railway is usually far from complete when it is opened for operation. The progress from crude, cheap and unsatisfactory construction, characterized by light iron rails, single tracks, heavy grades, and curves of short radii, to well-ballasted, level, multiple-track roadways composed of steel rails weighing often 100 pounds per yard has been accomplished during the working life of most American railways. To assume that the expenditures prior to the commencement of operation represent the total capital actually invested in such a railway is inadequate and unjust. Charges of stock watering are very frequently based upon the fact that it has seemed proper to railway managers to expend earnings upon improvements rather than to distribute them among investors and to satisfy the latter by issuing to them additional securities representing the amount of such expenditures. In other cases it has been impossible to induce capitalists to undertake the construction of a new line without conceding the privilege of purchasing its securities at less than their par value just as a merchant desiring to extend his business may secure the additional capital necessary by having his notes discounted. It would seem that the expense of such discounts on railway capital has been legitimately incurred. It is also to be remembered that whatever amount of securities may have been issued independently of actual expenditures has been to an extent, now undiscoverable, offset by the wiping out of securities incident to reorganization and foreclosure proceedings.

A very similar discussion purporting to be aimed at discovering the present value of railways assumes that this is to be ascertained by calculating the cost of duplicating existing lines. Though unsatisfactory from a scientific standpoint there would be little harm in this assumption were it not customary to omit from the supposed cost of duplication all but the bare expense of obtaining a fairly level roadway and placing upon it ties and rails. Expenditures for yards and terminals in large cities where land is costly, for constructing stations, for equipment, for signaling apparatus and for many other necessary purposes are usually omitted.

It is difficult to find reasonable justification for the expenditure of time and energy in these discussions. The amount which the public has to pay for transportation by rail is absolutely independent of capitalization except in so far as the securities represent actual investments. Relative par values and different classes of securities serve to determine the distribution of interest and dividends among capitalists who have invested under different conditions and, having accepted different hazards, are justly entitled to receive varying returns. The aggregate amount of these returns will in the long run inevitably be proportional to the investments and their rate will be determined by the rates prevalent in other enterprises, and the degree of risk assumed in the one in question. Wherever doubt and uncertainty affect their operations the proverbial timidity among capitalists causes the desertion of the field by the more cautious, leaving the business to those who are willing to adventure against great odds if assured of considerable gains in the event of success. Large profits are the inevitable consequences of large risks, and just as the keeper of a gambling establishment invariably insists that the law of chance shall give him a constant percentage of advantage in every game which he permits, so the speculator demands that in the long run the total profits of his successes shall be larger by a definite ratio than the total of his losses. Though it is undoubtedly true that the short-sightedness or the recklessness of individual speculators may result in financial ruin to themselves it is equally certain that considering them as a class they are able to make their demand for a balance of profits commensurate with the risks which they assume highly effective. Single railways may prove unprofitable, but that in the long run the railways of a developing nation must be profitable to investors is not open to doubt. The rate of profit will be determined by the conditions attending such investments, and these conditions are in a very large degree created by public sentiment and the legislative attitude which it imposes.

CHAPTER IV.

INCOME AND EXPENDITURE.

The annual gross earnings of the railways of the United States have, during recent years, varied within small percentages of twelve thousand millions of dollars, or, expressed comparatively, about one dollar in every ten of the aggregate value of the products of the farms and factories of the country has been devoted to the remuneration of the capital and labor employed in transportation. The following statement shows the income of the railways during the year ending with June 30, 1897, and its distribution among the different items of expenditure:

INCOME.

From passenger service—
Passenger revenue	$251,135,927	
Mail revenue	33,754,466	
Express revenue	24,901,066	
Other revenue	6,629,980	
		$316,421,439
From freight service—		
Freight revenue	$772,849,314	
Other revenue	4,209,657	
		$777,058,971
Other earnings from operation		28,609,363
Total from operation		$1,122,089,773
From other sources		125,090,010
Total		$1,247,179,783

EXPENDITURE.

Operating expenses—
Wages and salaries	$465,601,581	
Other expenses	286,923,183	
		$752,524,764
Taxes		43,137,844

Fixed charges—
Interest on funded debt *$247,880,230
Interest on current liabilities 7,844,336
Rents 87,505,302
Other charges 27,029,801
                                                $370,259,669
Dividends 87,110,599
Other payments from net income............... 267,390

Total $1,253.300,266
Deficit, to be deducted........................ 6,120,483

Balance (actual expenditure)................. $1,247,179,783

*Amount accrued during year. The amount actually paid from the year's income was probably less by about the amount of the deficit shown in the statement.

The foregoing statement throws useful light upon the revenue-producing power of the present body of railway rates, and may aid the thoughtful in determining whether it is justly charged that the earnings of American railways are excessive and extortionate. It shows that 37.3 per cent. of the total railway income, or 41.5 per cent. if that from other sources than operation, which is nearly all a bookkeeping duplication resulting from financial transactions among railway corporations themselves, is disregarded, was paid directly to employes in exchange for their labor; that 23.0 per cent. on the former and 25.5 per cent. on the latter basis was required to meet other operating expenses, most of which ultimately must have been paid for labor in some form; that more than 3.5 per cent. was paid to the various state and local governments for taxes, and that only 27.0 per cent., of which more than three-quarters was expended as interest on debt, was available for payments to investors. The total payment to investors amounted therefore to 2.91 per cent. on the aggregate capitalization, including unfunded debt, or, if the latter and its interest are excluded, to 3.09 per cent. The average rate of interest on funded debt was 4.70 per cent., and of dividends on stock 1.62 per cent. Stock having a par value of $3,761,092,277, or 70.1 per cent. of the total amount outstanding, received no dividends. Of the total capitalization, exclusive of equipment trust obligations, stocks and bonds, with a par value of $4,629,043,117, or 43.7 per cent., received neither dividends nor interest.

Operating expenses may also be classified with regard to the purposes for which they are incurred, as shown in the following statement, which relates to the fiscal year ending with June 30, 1897:

Expenditures for—	Amount.	Per cent. of total.
Maintenance of way and structures......	$159,434,403	21.22
Maintenance of equipment.............	122,762,358	16.34
Conducting transportation	432,525,862	57.58
General expenses	36,481,269	4.86
Total	$751,203,892	100.00
Unclassified (25 roads)	1,320,872	....
Total	$752,524,764	....

Apparently these expenditures should bear a somewhat constant relation to each other, and any considerable reduction of the proportionate allotments for those purposes which tend to protect the lives and property of the traveling and shipping public must be disadvantageous to the patrons of the railway system. Experience has shown that a sudden decrease in railway earnings will usually result in restricting the amounts available for keeping the means of transportation in good condition. Repairs and renewals can generally be postponed, though not without lessening the safety of travel and increasing the final expenditures for those purposes. Comparisons between the fiscal years 1893 and 1894 illustrate this tendency. The total movement of freight traffic during 1894 was, measured in ton miles, 16.5 per cent. less than during the previous year, and the low rates and heavy traffic caused by the Columbian Exposition barely sufficed to prevent a decline in the total volume of passenger business. Under these circumstances the total income from operation declined to $1,073,361,797, which was $147,390,077, or 12.1 per cent., lower than during the previous year; and as taxes and fixed charges remained substantially unchanged, and even dividends yield somewhat slowly to a decline in income, it became necessary to reduce quite materially the cost of operation. The reduction actually effected amounted to $96,506,977, or 11.7 per cent. of the expenses incurred for operation during 1893. Of this amount 26.6 per cent. was taken from the cost of maintenance of way and structures, which was reduced 15.1 per cent.; 24.9 per cent. from maintenance of equipment, reduced 17.5 per cent.; 42.5 per cent. from conducting transportation, reduced 9.4 per cent., and 6.0 per cent. from general expenses, reduced 6.8 per cent. These percentages should be compared with those in the table showing the relative importance of the several classes of expenditures. The manner in which these reductions were secured, in part at least, is indicated by the fact that the number of employes on June 30, 1894, was 93,994, or 10.8 per cent. less than twelve months previously. The reduction affected all classes of employes, but was greatest in the case of those

engaged in maintaining the character of roadway, structures and equipment.. The decrease, per 100 miles of
line, in the number of employes assigned to maintenance of way and structures was 18.5 per cent.; to maintenance of equipment, 16.5 per cent.; to general administration, 14.3 per cent., and to conducting transportation, 11.1 per cent. That there must have been a
decrease in the safety of travel and traffic is evident from
the fact that the number of section foremen and other
trackmen per 100 miles of line was reduced from 124
in 1893 to 102 in 1894.

CHAPTER V.

THE DECLINE IN CHARGES.

No other incident of the rapid development of railway facilities in the United States during the period subsequent to the war for the preservation of the Union is so thoroughly characteristic as the progressive reduction in the charges for the transportation services which they perform. The most reliable statistics that are available indicate that the average rate per passenger per mile collected by the railways during the year 1871 was, reduced to a gold basis, 2.632 cents. The average during 1881 was 2.446 cents; during 1891, 2.142 cents, and during 1896, 2.019 cents. Though the reduction in actual charges during a quarter of a century is seen to have been more than 23 per cent., it can by no means be adequately measured by statistics, for the services rendered in exchange for the money paid by passengers have varied in favor of the latter in every important element except that of distance. The dollar which purchases transportation in a train provided with automatic couplers and air brakes, traversing at a modern rate of speed a track of Bessemer steel rails weighing 100 pounds to the yard, and guarded by block signaling apparatus, buys vastly more than did a dollar paid for transportation under the conditions which existed but one or two decades ago.

With regard to freight traffic, the substantial identity in the services rendered at different periods which is necessary in order to warrant comparisons among the rates charged is, in spite of much improvement in speed and safety, more satisfactorily approximated. The average rate per ton of freight per mile carried measured in gold was 1.925 cents during 1867, 1.286 cents during 1877, 0.984 cent during 1887, and 0.806 cent during 1896, the decline during the three decades amounting to 58 per cent. In consequence of this reduction the average charge per ton of freight during 1896 was but $1.03⅜, though the average distance carried was 124½ miles, while during 1867 the average payment was $1.69¼ for a distance of 101¼ miles.

As the mere statement of these reductions may not afford an adequate estimate of their importance, it may be well to present a few comparisons. The average payment for railway transportation during 1896 by each man, woman and child in the United States was $14.48. Had it been possible for the railways to collect rates averaging as high per passenger per mile as those paid during 1871 and as high per ton of freight per mile as those of 1867 the railway transportation tax per capita would have been 111 per cent. greater, or $30.57. At the average rates of 1871 the passenger business of 1896 would have produced $79,990,414 more than it did produce, and at the average rates of 1867 the freight traffic of 1896 would have produced $1,066,724,352 more than was collected. In other words, the aggregate gross revenue from operation, which was $1,150,169,376, would have been nearly doubled. If the comparison is restricted to the charges during the last decade, it is found that at the average rates of 1887 the passenger business of the railways during 1896 would have been worth to them $29,490,756 more and the freight traffic $169,684,481 more than was actually collected, making a total saving to the people, through reduced charges, of $199,175,237, or about $2.79 per capita. It is interesting to observe that the latter amount is equal to about six times the annual interest on the national debt and exceeds considerably the customs revenues of the Federal Government for any fiscal year since 1891. It is two and one-quarter times as much as was paid in dividends during 1896 to all of the stockholders of the railways of the United States and but 20 per cent. less than the interest paid on their funded debt. Had it been collected and divided among the owners of railway securities it would have added 1.88 per cent. of the entire capitalization of the railways to the returns to investors, but contributed by the latter, as it was, to the people it was sufficient to pay at current rates for moving 9,865,043,933 passengers or 24,711,567,866 tons of freight one mile. It would have paid for carrying 386,-864,468 passengers 25.5 miles, which was the average distance traveled, or 198,534,328 tons of freight 124.47 miles, which was the average distance traversed by each ton of freight.

The obvious fact that no such increase in railway business as has taken place would have been possible unless accompanied by a substantial decrease in rates does not impair the value of this estimate, for the extension in the use of transportation facilities measures the increased efficiency in the organization of productive industry which has been secured through territorial division of labor which, fostered by the elimination of such a large portion of the former cost of exchanging the products of widely separated regions, is a direct consequence of cheapening transportation.

It is significant that the reductions described have not been confined to any particular locality, but have been distributed with substantial impartiality throughout the entire country. The following table shows the average rates per passenger and per ton of freight per mile charged during 1890 and 1896 in each of the ten groups adopted by the Statistician to the Interstate Commerce Commission for the classification of railway statistics:

AVERAGE RATES PER MILE IN CENTS.

Group.	Per passenger.		Per ton of freight.	
	1890.	1896.	1890.	1896.
I	1.912	1.839	1.373	1.213
II	2.029	1.834	.828	.672
III	2.199	2.020	.695	.618
IV	2.481	2.159	.844	.660
V	2.465	2.173	1.061	.886
VI	2.226	2.181	.961	.917
VII	2.452	2.564	1.360	1.121
VIII	2.268	2.188	1.152	1.055
IX	2.583	2.298	1.303	1.118
X	2.308	2.131	1.651	1.254

It is thus seen that in every group but one, that including Arkansas, Kansas, Oklahoma, Indian Territory, a small portion of Northern New Mexico, nearly all of Colorado, and the Southern half of Missouri, passenger rates have declined and that freight rates are considerably lower in every group. According to the latest data published by the Interstate Commerce Commission the entire balance over operating expenses of the gross earnings during the fiscal year 1897 of the railways in groups seven, nine and ten was not sufficient to meet their fixed charges had nothing whatever been allotted for dividends.

Averages such as those which have been cited, representing respectively the aggregate railway passenger and freight traffic of the entire country, or of extensive districts, constitute the most satisfactory means of measuring the changes in the charges for railway services because they neither exclude local traffic nor give to rates made under the competition of rival roads the excessive importance sometimes apparent in efforts to represent the reductions by comparisons among charges applied at different times to particular commodities or between particular points. Comparisons of the latter class, however, have their value and may not be neglected. Probably the rates affecting the greatest amount of traffic are those charged between New York and Chicago. This is not merely because these are the most populous of American cities, nor is it attributable solely to their importance as distributing centers or as commercial gateways through which trade seeks access to regions rich in agricultural resources or abounding in manufacturing industries, but principally on account of the arrangement by which rates between them have become the basis of charges on a vast amount of traffic which neither originates at nor passes through either of them.

During 1867 the average rates in gold on dry goods, cotton piece goods, boots and shoes, tea and drugs from New York to Chicago were $1.37 per 100 pounds. During 1897 the average rate on cotton piece goods was 50 cents, and on each of the other articles 75 cents per 100 pounds. The average rate on sugar in carloads between the same places and during the same period declined from 60 to 24, and that on common soap from 93 to 25 cents per 100 pounds. During 1858 it cost 38.61 cents per bushel to ship wheat from Chicago to New York; during 1868, 27.09 cents; during 1878, 17.56 cents; during 1888, 14.50 cents, and during 1896, 12.50 cents. From 1872 to 1896 the average rate on dressed beef, Chicago to New York, declined from 81 to 45 cents; that on packed meats from Cincinnati to New York from 44.59 cents to 26 cents per 100 pounds. The Lehigh Valley Railroad received 1.746 cents per ton per mile for carrying anthracite coal during 1869, 1.093 cents during 1879, 0.967 cent during 1889, and 0.712 cent during 1897. Compressed cotton, carried from Memphis to Boston during 1880 for 79 cents, was taken during 1897 at rates averaging 55 cents per 100 pounds.

The instances of reductions are so numerous that the labor of citing them is entirely one of selection, and it is not too much to say that it is impossible to find any important article of commerce on which the rates charged by railways have remained without substantial reduction during any very considerable period.

CHAPTER VI.

RATES AND PRICES.

In the preceding chapter it was shown that from 1867 to 1896 the average rate per ton of freight per mile transported charged by the railways of the United States declined not less than 58 per cent., from 1.925 cents to 0.806 cent, the average of the earlier year having been made comparable with that for 1896 by being reduced from 2.678 cents, the amount actually paid in currency, to the equivalent of the latter in gold. It is now proposed to compare the decline in railway charges with contemporaneous changes in the prices of the principal articles commonly shipped by rail.

The three leading cereal products of the United States constitute a very important portion of the eastward bound traffic of our principal railways. For the purpose of the following comparison the average of the farm prices of each of these cereals for the six years from 1867 to 1872, inclusive, has been considered as 100 per cent. and made the basis from which to calculate the percentage of the prices of other years. Similarly the average of the rates per ton per mile of the years from 1867 to 1872 has been made the basis of the percentages in the column headed "freight rates."

Year.	Corn	Prices Wheat	Oats	Freight. rates.
Average 1867 to 1872.	100	100	100	100
1867............	117	134	116	105
1872............	73	103	78	101
1877............	72	98	74	70
1882............	100	81	98	60
1887............	91	63	80	54
1892............	81	58	83	49
1896............	44	67	.49	44

The foregoing figures show that during every year subsequent to that used as the basis of the calculation the average of the freight rates charged throughout the country has constituted a smaller percentage of the average for the first six years than has the average farm price of either of the products named, with the single exception of corn during 1896, when the unusually abundant production resulted in an abnormally low price. The table also develops an interesting and important difference between the decline in prices and that in freight rates. Though the former has been marked, and may not be attributed solely to temporary causes, the violent fluctuations from year to year show the consequences of changes in the quantities harvested and that prices are ultimately effectually controlled by cost of production. The decline in rates, on the other hand, has been without interruption and notably regular. The consequence is that the averages of any series of years which can be selected will show that a greater advantage has accrued to the shipper of farm products than is indicated by a merely superficial examination of the figures in the table.

In the following statement the average rates on wheat shipped from Chicago to New York via the all-rail lines are compared with contemporaneous export prices for the purpose of ascertaining how many bushels could be transported between those points at successive periods and the freight paid by the delivery to the carrier of one bushel of the grain or its equivalent in cash:

WHEAT.

Year.	Export price per bushel.	Rate Chicago to New York, per bushel. Cents.	Number of bushels carried for price of one bushel
1867	$0.92	32.38	2.84
1872	1.31	31.13	4.21
1877	1.12	19.56	5.73
1882	1.19	14.47	8.22
1887	.89	15.75	5.65
1892	1.03	13.80	7.46
1897	.75	12.50	6.00

The foregoing figures show that during 1867 the carriers were given the equivalent of one bushel out of every 2.84 bushels which they moved from Chicago to the Atlantic seaboard as compensation for their services; that during no subsequent year shown have they received as large a proportion of the value of the grain transported, and that during the year 1897 they took but one bushel out of every six transported. As rates, Chicago to New York, are the basis upon which the charges applied to nearly every bushel of the surplus wheat crop of the country are computed, it is evident that this explains in a very large degree the steadily increasing proportion of the full export prices of his products received by the farmer.

Several of the principal anthracite coal carrying railways segregate the tonnage and revenue of the latter from their general business in their accounts, and data are thus available for valuable comparisons. The average rate per ton of coal carried one mile during 1889 by the Lehigh Valley Railroad was 1.746 cents for a ton of 2000 pounds, or 1.956 cents for a ton of 2240 pounds. At the same time the average price of anthracite coal in Philadelphia was $3.92 per long ton. Comparing these averages it is evident that, supposing transportation to commence at Philadelphia, the cost of movement would have more than equalled the original value of the coal when the latter passed beyond a radius of 200 miles from the starting-point. During the year 1879 the relation between prices and rates permitted a radius of 221 miles before the cost of coal more than doubled; during 1889 the radius was 373, and during 1897 it was 439 miles.

Comparisons between the average rate of wages and railway rates, made possible by means of the elaborate investigation into the course of prices and wages, conducted during 1891 by the Committee on Finance of the United States Senate, show that the power of a definite amount of labor to purchase transportation vastly increased during the period studied. According to the report of that investigation the same quantity of labor which, taking an average of the entire country for six years from 1867 to 1872, inclusive, was compensated by the payment of $100 in gold as wages, received during 1877, $101; during 1882, $114; during 1887, $117, and during 1891, $126. The course of freight rates furnishes a marked contrast. During 1867 to 1872 the workingman's $100 in gold would pay for moving 4333 passengers, or 5470 tons of freight one mile. The wages received for the same amount of labor during 1877 would have paid for moving 4109 passengers or 7854 tons of freight one mile; during 1882, 4768 passengers or 10,345 tons of freight; during 1887, 5212 passengers or 11,890 tons of freight; and during 1891, 5882 passengers or 14,078 tons of freight might have been moved one mile for an amount equaling the average compensation received by workingmen for the same quantity of labor for which $100 in gold was received during the years 1867 to 1872, inclusive. It is to be regretted that data for later comparisons are not available.

Without adducing further evidence, which would be merely cumulative, it seems legitimate to conclude that the purchasing power of labor when applied to the transportation of either persons or property, and that of products when applied to their own transportation, have materially increased during the last three decades. The most notable economic result of this change in the relation between the cost of movement and the primary cost of production is an increase in the average radius of the regions from which particular communities can profitably purchase the products needed for local consumption, and as this, by permitting a greater range of selection, not infrequently brings into cultivation land of greater productivity, it has been accompanied in many instances by a rise in the margin of cultivation and a consequent reduction in the average cost of production of the form utilities required. In other words, the progressive decrease in transportation charges, whether measured in dollars, in labor, or in commodities, has permitted a very desirable specialization of the industrial functions of different regions, the assignment to each particular locality of the share in production for which its capacity is greatest, and has materially increased the productivity of human labor.

CHAPTER VII.

CAUSES OF THE DECLINE IN CHARGES.

A thorough and impartial examination of the circumstances attending the decline in the average charges for railway services which has been illustrated and discussed in the last two chapters of this work will doubtless show that the efficient cause of rate reductions has been the competition of rival commercial centers, markets and producing regions, and that the *pseudo-*competition among railway routes connecting the same localities, though producing reductions, more or less permanent, in through or competitive charges, has actually tended to prevent a progressive decline in the average rate which represents local as well as through traffic. The distinction between these forms, both of which unquestionably affect railway charges, is of primary importance, particularly as the popular belief that the so-called competition of the second form has substantial regulative effect on railway charges has been the prolific parent of much unwise and positively detrimental restrictive legislation; but the discussion of competition should be preceded by that of certain other factors of the phenomenon of declining charges, and will be deferred for another chapter, because, however efficient it may have been, in either of its forms, in securing to the public the benefits of cheaper transportation, it would have been impotent to produce permanent reductions of the magnitude observed had not its operation been accompanied by other circumstances which have permitted the *quasi*-public corporations engaged in railway transportation to furnish their services at lower cost to themselves.

The increasing use of transportation facilities is both a cause and a result of the reduced prices at which those facilities have become available for public use. The cost of a railway which moves 750,000 tons one mile per mile of its length is not necessarily materially greater than that of another road the traffic of which is relatively meager, and the cost of maintenance of way, structures and equipment, of conducting transportation, and of administration by no means varies in the same ratio as traffic. The obvious consequence is that each increment of traffic permits the distribution of expenses among an increased number of tons and of ton-miles, and thus reduces the average amount of cost assignable to each. This is what is meant by the "law of increasing returns," which, as applied to railway business, signifies that without changes in rates increased traffic tends to augment gross earnings faster than expenses and consequently to produce increased profits. The absence of such enhanced profits is due to the fact that the benefits of the savings per unit of service permitted by increasing traffic have accrued to railway patrons through reduced charges instead of the owners of railway securities through higher rates of interest and of dividends. During the year 1867 railways having a total length of 15,651 miles, or 42 per cent. of the entire mileage then in operation, carried an aggregate traffic averaging 279,712 tons one mile per mile of line. These roads included those in the most developed sections of the country and having the densest traffic, so that the average for the entire country was probably considerably lower. In 1872 the average was 331,958 on 61 per cent. of the railway mileage; in 1877, 345,773 on 77 per cent.; in 1882, 457,016 on 80 per cent.; in 1887, 513,513 on 78 per cent., and in 1892 and 1896, 543,365 and 523,832, respectively, on practically the total mileage of the United States. The decrease from 1892 to 1896 is attributable to the general business depression, and the fact that it was accompanied by decreasing rather than increasing charges is due to the severe economies practice l and the almost universal impracticability of advancing railway rates.

The efficiency of railway service has steadily increased during the last two or three decades through physical improvements of great importance. The substitution of steel for iron as the material from which rails are made, and in later years the use of heavier rails, have been greatly fostered by the progressive reduction in the cost of rails attributable to improvements in steel and rail-making processes. The manufacture of steel rails in commercial quantities in the United States began in 1867, and the average price during that year was $120.12 per ton. In 1880 the price had declined to $67.50, and 29 per cent. of the railway track in the country was composed of steel rails. The price in 1890 was $31.75 and 80 per cent. of all track was of steel; in 1896 the price was $28 and but 12 per cent. of the total trackage remained of iron. Heavier locomotives, larger cars, and faster and larger trains are secondary consequences of the reduced cost of steel rails, and these increase the efficiency of the train as a machine for moving commodities. The average number of tons carried one mile per mile run by freight trains was 80.77

in 1867, 134.83 in 1880, 175.12 in 1890, and 198.81 in 1896, and these figures do much to explain the ability of railways to reduce the average charge per ton from $1.69 to $1.03, and per ton-mile from 1.925 cents to 0.806 cent.

It would be impracticable in the space allotted to enumerate even the more important of the administrative economies which have been effected, but attention should be directed to the consequences of those tendencies toward the unification of the railways which have rendered their services cheaper, and at the same time more satisfactory and valuable. Railway associations, agreements in regard to the establishment and maintenance of rates or the character and conditions of services to be performed; the three great freight classifications, each prevailing uniformly with regard to the traffic of extensive sections of the country; the interchange of cars which permits shipments to traverse many roads without transfer from car to car; through rates, routes and billing arrangements, are all phases of a development which, in spite of unwise and hindering legislation, is making a railway *system* out of theoretically independent and rival railway corporations. The processes of this development cannot, with the data which are now available, be shown statistically, but its principal incidents are familiar to every intelligent observer.

Having shown some of the causes which have permitted reductions in rates, it will not be out of place to emphasize the fact that such reductions have not been accomplished through any decrease in the average rate of wages paid to employes. According to the latest

report of the Statistician to the Interstate Commerce
Commission, $465,601,581, or 62 per cent. of the aggre-
gate operating expenses of the railways of the United
States during the year ending with June 30, 1897, was
paid to employes, and of this amount less than three
per cent. was paid to general officers. The previous report gave the average per diem rate of compensation of
each class of employes during each year from 1892 to
1896, inclusive, and it is interesting to observe that the
business depression which during 1893 and 1894 forced
such a large proportion of the railways into insolvency
did not result in any material reduction in the rates of
wages paid.

The following statement shows some of these rates:

Year.	Enginemen.	Firemen.	Con-ductors	Train-men, not conductors.	Track-men.	Switchmen, flagmen and brakesmen.
1892.......	$3.68	$2.07	$3.07	$1.89	$1.22	$1.78
1893.......	3.66	2.04	3.08	1.91	1.22	1.80
1894.......	3.61	2.03	3.04	1.89	1.18	1.75
1895.......	3.65	2.05	3.04	1.90	1.17	1.75
1896.......	3.65	2.06	3.05	1.90	1.17	1.74

Satisfactory statistics of wages paid during an extensive period are not available for the whole country, but
the data which have been preserved afford unmistakable
evidence of an upward movement in the wages of railway labor almost as extensive and quite as distinct as
the downward tendency in rates.

CHAPTER VIII.

COMPETITION AMONG RAILWAYS AND THE DECLINE IN CHARGES.

The substantial savings in the cost of moving traffic indicated in the last chapter of this work, so far as they could have been effected in the absence of the increased traffic resulting from lower charges, would, had they been unaccompanied by decreasing rates, have accrued to the benefit of the owners, managers, and employes of railway properties in the form of enhanced compensation for the capital and labor employed in the business of transportation. That they have not done so, but, together with another sum subtracted through actual reductions in the rates of interest and dividends on railway capital from the incomes of investors in such properties, have been diverted to the pockets of passengers and shippers, has resulted from well-defined commercial laws which should be thoroughly understood.

As has been suggested, two forms of competition, not at all interdependent, affect and, in some instances, control the charges exacted for railway services. Competition among railways offering to perform identical services constitutes the form first to attract the notice of superficial investigators, and may operate so as to reduce charges between localities served by two or more railways, but as it cannot be maintained effectively without certain considerable expenditures for operation, which would otherwise be unnecessary, it must, if indulged in extensively, impose bankruptcy upon the railways resorting to it unless additional revenue sufficient to compensate for the reductions and extraordinary expenditures in connection with competitive traffic is collected from local traffic. As the community served must eventually pay, in one way or another, for whatever transportation it receives, such competition actually tends to limit, if not entirely to prevent, any reduction in the average rate collected from all traffic, and also as may be mentioned incidentally to produce unjust discriminations against localities served by but one carrier.

Although the social consequences of unjust discriminations among the purchasers of transportation are unquestionably much more to be feared than any conjectural danger of excessive rates, an apparently plausible defense of legislative attempts, such as the anti-pooling clause of the Interstate Commerce law, to enforce competition among railways is based upon the contention that the decline in charges has resulted from such competition. The too frequently undetected assumption that coincidence of time and place establish a relation as between cause and effect thus constitutes the foundation of a structure which under closer scrutiny crumbles to the ground. Careful investigation of the incidents of the decline in charges shows clearly that it has resulted from causes wholly extraneous to the railway system, except in so far as the enlightened perception on the part of the officials having charge of railways that the permanent success of those properties must be based upon the development of the respective territories contiguous and tributary to their lines, and that such development is dependent upon reasonable transportation rates, can be considered an intrinsic cause. Before passing to the consideration of the competition of producers and markets, it will be useful to point out some of the wasteful expenditures resulting from that form of competition which is operative only at the relatively few points served by two or more railways.

Authentic statistics of the amounts paid by rival lines as commissions for securing business are very difficult to obtain, as the success of such practices depends very largely upon the degree of secrecy that can be attained. The Interstate Commerce Commission was able, however, to ascertain that nine roads paid out an aggregate sum of more than one million dollars in a single year as commissions on passenger business alone, and it has been stated on reliable authority that as much as $20.70 has been paid to secure a single second-class passenger from Chicago to San Francisco. The multitude of outside agencies and traveling agents maintained solely for the purpose of securing business for their respective lines that might otherwise traverse those of their competitors involves an expenditure so great, even during periods of comparative harmony, that it has been necessary to restrict their number by contract. The agreement now in force limits to eight the number of passenger agencies that may be maintained in New York City by each of the nine roads competing for westward bound traffic. As it is a fact of ordinary observation that such agencies always cluster in particular portions of a city and around particular corners, it is obvious that a system of joint agencies would afford the public equal accommodation at lower cost.

During the periods of unbridled competition, popularly known as "rate wars," each participating carrier has its freight and passenger agents in every important city in the country at a total expense for rents, clerk hire, advertising, etc. that must be enormous. Four roads operating westward from Chicago are known to have expended $1,283,585 for outside agencies and advertising in a single year, during which rates were fairly maintained, while during an equal period one road terminating at New York expended $871,291 for similar purposes. The competition of long, circuitous and commercially illegitimate routes for traffic that would naturally traverse cheaper and more direct lines is another gross extravagance too frequently observed. Mr. Firth, president of the Erie and Western Transportation Company, whose wide experience guarantees the accuracy of any assertion he may make, has recently stated that:

"Illegitimate business is always the pride of the average traffic manager. To secure a share of some competitive business, not naturally or fairly belonging to a carrying line, always appears to inspire heroic efforts and to be regarded as meriting special commendation."

Illustrations are numerous. Between St. Paul and Chicago, with a short line distance of 373 miles, traffic is carried by a line 734 miles in length. From Chicago to New York twenty-one routes ranging from 912 to 1376 miles compete for traffic, while between Omaha and San Francisco there are five, of which the shortest is 1865 and the longest 2724 miles. Besides the numerous regular and "tramp" steamships available for shipments from New York to New Orleans, more than ninety all-rail lines are each actively seeking a share in the business. The most direct of these is 1340 miles in length or 711 miles shorter than the longest. As an example of the waste of competitive train service, it is not necessary to add to the bare statement that forty-four trains leave Chicago for New York every day, and that similar duplication of service exists wherever the same cities are connected by competing railways. No intelligent student of transportation doubts that whenever it becomes possible, by means of the adoption of wiser principles as the basis of regulative legislation, to eliminate from the cost of railway operation these economically useless and wasteful expenditures, now reluctantly incurred in consequence of vicious laws which are intended to perpetuate competition among railway carriers, the saving thus effected will accrue to the benefit of the general public through further reductions in rates which will thus be permitted to result from the action and interaction of commercial forces.

The failure of competition among railways is not attributable to causes which invalidate the competitive principle as applied to general business and within its proper sphere, but to the fact that modern conditions of land transportation are such that competition, in the ordinary sense, among the agencies employed is impracticable. Far the greater number of railway stations are dependent upon single railway lines, and the vastly larger portion of railway traffic has no alternative route available. To these stations and this traffic the relation of the railway corporation is that of a monopoly, and from them the latter can and will, within certain limits and with certain qualifications which are not material to the present discussion, recoup all losses that may be sustained at the comparatively few points and in carrying the relatively inconsiderable traffic, with regard to which there is actual competition. It is to preserve the latter, useless and baneful as it is, that obstacles to the full operation of competition among producers have been interposed by provisions forbidding the consolidation of parallel lines frequently found in state constitutions, acts of state legislatures and corporate charters, by the anti-pooling clause of the Interstate Commerce law, and, accepting the interpretation of the anti-trust law adopted by the United States Supreme Court in the Trans-Missouri case, by the anti-trust law.

CHAPTER IX.

COMPETITION AMONG PRODUCERS AND THE DECLINE IN CHARGES.

The salient facts so far developed in this work are that the charges for railway transportation have, during the last three decades, continuously and materially declined; that this decline, though accompanied by a general lowering of the prices of commodities, has been much greater than that in the prices of most important articles of traffic, and has been contemporaneous with an actual advance in rates of wages; that increased traffic and better methods have resulted in a lowered average cost, per unit of service, of furnishing the public with railway facilities and conducting railway transportation; and that competition among railways serving the same localities not only does not explain the diversion of the sums so saved from the pockets of railway owners, managers and employes to those of travelers and shippers, but that there is abundant evidence that it has hindered the reduction of the average rates for the movement of passengers and freight.

It has already been suggested that competition among markets and producers does furnish the explanation sought, and that the substantial reductions in average rates which have taken place during the prevalence of competition among carriers, and in spite of the wasteful expenditures and losses incident thereto, are due principally to the fact that these forms of competition have operated contemporaneously and to the more extensive application and superior efficiency of compe-

tition among railway patrons for the privilege of buying
or selling in particular regions.

The quantity of any commodity which a particular
community will purchase at a particular price during
any period is definite and, within certain limits, ascertainable. With regard to most commodities, lowering
the price will increase the quantity consumed, and
raising the price will decrease it, while the price itself
equals, in the long run, the cost of the last increment
of the supply for which there is an effective demand.
Transportation charges are properly regarded as constituting a portion of the cost of production of the commodities moved because production is not an accomplished fact until products have become available at the
points where they are required for consumption.
Thus the radius of the region in which the products
of a particular locality can be marketed with profit
is determined by the cost of production at that
place and the rates charged for transportation over
the routes available for moving those products.
Each producer, desiring to extend his business or
increase his income, perceives that in order to
secure a wider market or to obtain greater profits in
those already reached, it is only necessary to obtain
lower rates on his shipments. Any concession of this
kind made to one shipper invariably inspires demands
for similar reductions not only on the part of competitors in the same locality, but others in distant regions
whose products meet with those of the locality affected
by the initial reduction in a common market. Whether
salt from Kansas or from Michigan shall be consumed
in certain sections of Iowa and other Western states is

determined by the relation between the rates imposed for transportation to the consuming region from the salt-producing sections of the former states.   Boots and shoes manufactured in Chicago or St. Louis meet with those from the Atlantic Seaboard on equal terms in every community to which the respective charges for transportation plus cost of production in each related locality produce equal sums, and not infrequently the manufacturer finds the former element more readily controllable than the latter.   The commercial rivalry of New York, Boston, Philadelphia and Baltimore, each seeking to add to the volume of its export trade, has been much more effective in inducing the present low rates for moving grain to those ports than the more or less continuous competition among the railways serving them.   A curious evidence of this fact is found in the negotiations which resulted in the final adoption of the differential relations among the charges to those ports which have remained unchanged since 1877.   These negotiations were preceded by a period of demoralized rates which was forced upon the railways by the commercial organizations of the respective ports, and they culminated in arbitration proceedings in which the questions involved were submitted to Messrs. Allen G. Thurman, Elihu B. Washburn and Thomas M. Cooley, none of whom had any connection with any railway corporation.   The railway companies expressly declined to participate in any way in the investigations and deliberations of this committee, except so far as to furnish it with any information which should be requested, and the numerous arguments heard and the testimony taken were all introduced by the commercial organizations of the interested cities, yet the railways accepted without hesitation the conclusions of the committee and have ever since acted in accordance therewith.   This arbitration having restricted the consequences of competition among the Atlantic ports, rates were for many years maintained with fair success, and the next radical reduction in charges applied to grain shipments to those ports was the result of their common desire to prevent the diversion of such shipments to Gulf ports.

Competing shippers in the same locality are always endeavoring to obtain more favorable rates than those accorded to their rivals, and though these may be, under present conditions, temporarily secret, they not infrequently lead to open reductions.   The use of particular commodities is often limited territorially by the freight charges from the points of production to those of consumption, and, when charges are too high on certain articles, substitutes produced nearer the points of consumption, or carried at lower freight rates, are frequently used.   The charges for passenger transportation also, by limiting the distance to which agents can be profitably sent and otherwise hindering personal communication, effectively prescribe the limits of profitable interchange of commodities, and interfere with the territorial division of labor.

In consequence of these facts the whole force of commercial competition, possibly the most tremendous product of modern industrial and economic organization, is arrayed in continuous effort to secure ever-cheapening transportation.   As a result railway charges tend unceasingly toward the lowest rates that will produce a revenue sufficient in the aggregate to meet operating expenses, including necessary repairs and renewals, and, in addition, return to capital the lowest recompense for which it can be procured. As the latter is at any time a definite sum, it is evident that expenses of operation constitute the only controllable element. Here is found a barrier which legislative attempts to secure and perpetuate railway competition have erected against further reductions in charges made possible by economies in operation.

Competition among producers would not, of course, be as effective as it is were it not supplemented by a condition, inseparable from the business of railway transportation, which makes the rates charged for railway services extremely vulnerable to demands supported by the commercial necessities of railway patrons. Capital in the form of railway facilities is not transferable to other industries, or even, except with regard to an insignificant fraction of the aggregate, to the same industry in other fields. Consequently the permanent prosperity of any railway corporation is dependent upon the development of the resources of the territory tributary to the lines which it operates, and as this development cannot be secured except through rates which are, both absolutely and relatively to charges from and to other regions, reasonable, the corporation whose officers attempt to impose unreasonable rates is certain to be unsuccessful. An active and intelligent perception of this fact has been a marked characteristic of American railway officials, and the instances in which they have hesitated to make rates low enough to permit the inauguration of new industries in suitable localities or the extension of those already in existence within economically profitable limits are few indeed.

It is, therefore, as a consequence of competition among producers, which affects practically all freight traffic, and not of that among railways, which can be controlling at relatively few points, that railway rates have declined so considerably. The reduction, in spite of the increase in the volume of traffic that has been its accompaniment, has exceeded that in the cost of operation, the latter having been unduly enhanced by the extravagant and wasteful expenditures required to maintain a *pseudo*-competition, the perpetuation of which has been imposed upon reluctant carriers by unwise and uneconomic legislation. Thus, while rates have progressively declined and traffic per mile of line rapidly increased, the percentage of operating expenses to gross earnings has, in spite of the law of increasing returns, continuously increased. The return to capital invested in railway facilities cannot in fairness be further reduced, and if it could such a course would merely retard the adequate development of those facilities. Railway rates are, under present conditions of operation, too low, and if they are to be maintained on the present level or further reductions asked, the unfavorable conditions which result from unwise legislation should be removed.

CHAPTER X.

THE LAW OF INCREASING RETURNS.

Certain industries, especially those in which the cost of operation is low in comparison with the original cost of the necessary plant, can augment their production within the capacity of the plant already in existence without increasing the amount of capital required or the cost of production in as large a proportion as the increase in production. The result is a lower average cost per unit of the product and, if prices are maintained at the former level, an increased ratio of profits upon the capital employed. Such industries are subject to the law of increasing returns which is, that, under the conditions described, the application of increased capital or labor augments production in a greater proportion than that of the necessary increment of expenditure to that formerly required, or of the added production to the former production. It is especially important not to forget that the accurate statement of the law does not indicate increased rates of profit unless prices remain constant, for in practice each increment of production is usually followed by a reduction in the price obtainable per unit, and it is always possible that this reduction may completely offset the reduction in cost due to the distribution of the expenses incurred for the establishment and operation of the plant among a larger number of units.

Probably no railway in the United States has ever carried during any considerable period as much traffic as it might have moved if utilized to its full capacity. A

particular track, train, locomotive, or car will seldom be
found to be performing all the transportation services
of which it is capable. These facts, which bring the ·
business of railway transportation within the operation
of the law of increasing returns, are quite generally understood, but the fact that this law will not secure for
the carrier increased or even undiminished returns in
the face of indefinitely decreasing rates, is frequently
neglected, and it is assumed by a too numerous section
of the public and by many legislators that increased
traffic is, if not always, at least with very rare exceptions, accompanied by an increased rate of profit. Unfortunately for those who have invested in railway properties this is not the case, and the decrease in rates has
absorbed more than the decrease in cost of operation
which has resulted from increased traffic and the economies referred to in the seventh chapter of this work. In
spite of increasing traffic the gross earnings per mile of
line operated by the railways of the United States have
declined from $8086 in 1871, $7548 in 1881, and $6852
in 1891 to $6223 in 1896; while net earnings which in
1871 amounted to $2842 per mile of line, though in-
creasing slightly to $2930 in 1881, had decreased to
$2136 in 1891 and to $1837 in 1896. The temporary
increase no doubt indicates that the earlier reductions
were accompanied by economies in cost of operation per
unit of traffic that prevented a decline in net earnings,
while the rapid decrease of the last fifteen years shows
that it was found impossible permanently to keep down
the ratio of operating expenses to gross earnings. The
actual relation of the aggregate cost of operation to the
total gross earnings was as 65.08 per cent. in 1873 and

58.36 per cent. in 1880, the decline to the latter year
having been substantially regular. In 1885 the proportion had again risen to 65.12 per cent., in 1890 to
65.80 per cent., and in 1896 to 67.20 per cent. Dividends on capital stock averaged $1132 per mile of op-
erated road in 1871, $1004 in 1881, $542 in 1891, and
$450 in 1896; while interest on funded debt was $1242
in 1881, $1362 in 1891, and $1402 in 1896 per mile of
line. The total of these payments on capital was in
1881 $2246 per mile of line, in 1891 $1904, and in 1896
$1852. The slight increase in the interest payments
per mile of line is attributable to the increased proportion of bonded indebtedness in the capitalization of railways; but that this does not completely account for the
great fall in dividends is evident from the actual decrease in the total of payments per mile of line. The
average capitalization per mile of road having slightly
increased during the last three decades, it is evident
that increased traffic has not brought increased profits
to railway owners. One result of the facts just cited
is that the financial condition of many railways is not
sufficiently stable to carry them through even brief
periods of business depression. Doing business upon
an exceedingly narrow margin of profit during periods
of prosperity, they are unable to accumulate funds to
bear the expenses of temporarily unprofitable business,
while the commercial conditions in most cases make it
impracticable to compensate diminished traffic by increased charges per unit of service. Under these circumstances it is scarcely surprising that during the
panic years of 1884 and 1885 19,406 miles of railway
were placed in charge of receivers, or that during the

years 1892 and 1893 39,848 miles were similarly transferred to the control of the Federal Courts on account of their, at least temporary, insolvency. The par value of the capital of the railroads thus becoming bankrupt during 1884 and 1885 was $1,100,155,000, and during 1893 and 1894, $2,038,738,000. The foreclosures following receiverships are generally distributed more evenly over the years succeeding the periods of acute depression. During the four years from 1894 to 1897, inclusive, 38,879 miles of railway with capital having a par value of $2,748,847,000 were sold in foreclosure proceedings after having become unable to meet the interest upon their indebtedness.

It is evident from the foregoing that the law of increasing returns has not only failed to save railway corporations from the consequences of declining rates, but also that the rate of return on investments in railway properties has actually declined. These facts should not be lost sight of by those, not invariably dishonest, who advocate radical reductions in rates, and supplement their arguments by the contention that the adoption of their proposals will increase, or at least will not decrease, the profits of railway business. The bases of these claims are usually a fallacious application of the law of the increasing returns, in which the importance of constant rates or prices is ignored and an exaggerated statement of the elasticity of railway traffic.

While it is perfectly true that the movement of most articles of traffic can be stimulated by rate reductions, the increases possible are invariably strictly limited by the amounts of the reductions, and in many instances even extreme reductions would but slightly augment the volume of business. 'Passenger traffic, with the exception of suburban business, is but slightly susceptible of increase, and there are numerous articles of freight traffic which, either on account of the small proportion of freight charges to the total value or the limited requirements of consumers, could not be moved much more extensively than at present. For example, rates on clothing and boots and shoes are probably low enough to move, at the present time, nearly as large quantities of those commodities as would be shipped at the lowest conceivable charges. The same reason, together with the fact that there is no desire on the part of consumers for much greater supplies of those articles would probably render tea, coffee, sugar, salt, and many similar articles unresponsive to even the most radical rate reductions. In a future chapter the desirability, from the standpoint of the general public, of indefinite increases in the volume of traffic, which is so frequently taken for granted, will be discussed and an attempt made to define the cases in which transportation reduces the cost of production, and to show when it increases such cost and is consequently undesirable.

CHAPTER XI.

INCREASING USE OF RAILWAY FACILITIES.

Contemporaneous with the decline in the charges exacted for railway services, there has been an increase in the aggregate amount of transportation purchased by the people that is proportionally much greater than the increase of population during the same period. According to the report on Transportation of the Tenth Census, the fifty million persons then inhabiting the United States required of the railway facilities existing during 1880 the performance of services which, in the aggregate, were equivalent to moving 5,740,112,502 passengers and 32,348,848,693 tons of freight one mile. Ten years later, though population had increased to but, approximately, sixty-two and one-half millions, the railways carried 11,992,112,154 passengers and 79,172,-464,796 tons of freight one mile. Thus a growth of but 25 per cent. in the number of railway patrons was accompanied by an increase of 109 per cent. in the aggregate passenger movement, and of 144 per cent. in the total freight transportation.

The following table shows the relation between population and the aggregate railway transportation during the concluding year of each quinquennial period from 1867 to 1892 and during 1896:

| Year. | Number carried one mile per capita of population— | |
	Passengers.	Tons of freight.
1867	138	285
1872	161	517
1877	118	578
·882	179	949
1887	208	1,266
1892	204	1,349
1896	183	1,338

From the foregoing table it appears that the average amount of transportation performed by the railways for each man, woman and child in the United States has increased from carrying 138 passengers and 285 tons of freight one mile in 1867 to moving 183 passengers and 1338 tons of freight the same distance in 1896, or about 32 per cent. in the case of passengers and 369 per cent. in that of freight. The averages in question are based upon estimates of population prepared in the Treasury Department by the Government Actuary, and, while the latter are generally reasonably accurate, it is not impossible that the slight decrease in freight transportation per capita from 1892 to 1896 and a part of that in passenger movement are attributable to an overestimate of the population for the later year.

The increased utilization of railway facilities shown is not the result of diversion of traffic from lake, river, canal or ocean carriers, but represents an absolute increase in the aggregate transportation demanded by the people, for, while in a few instances river transportation has been rendered unprofitable by the competition of railways, the total movement of commodities over water routes has considerably increased during the period that has witnessed the extraordinary development of railway business which has been noted.   Domestic commerce being practically free from legislative interference, except in the few instances in which restraints are imposed in the exercise of the police powers of the several states, consumers have naturally sought to purchase their supplies and producers have vended their commodities in the markets, in each particular case, appearing to be most advantageous.   Similarly communities have been led, in seeking to satisfy the desires, as consumers, of their individual members with the least practicable expenditure of effort, to devote increasing proportions of their energies to particular industries from the conduct of which especially favorable results might be anticipated, and to depend upon exchanging the surplus products of such industries for necessaries and luxuries which might not be produced locally with approximately equal facility or profit.   Innumerable illustrations of the practical operation of the tendencies described might be cited.   Massachusetts, with a population which annually consumes the flour obtained from about ten million bushels of wheat, has practically ceased to produce that cereal, and secures its necessary supply of this important breadstuff by exchanging therefor a portion of the surplus products of its factories, the total output of which averages about $400 in annual value for each of the citizens of that commonwealth. The production and manufacture of raw wool and the manufacture and distribution of woolens and woolen goods afford an excellent example of the importance of the transportation factor in the modern industrial system.   During the last census year (1890) the six New England states contributed but 2.67 per cent. of the domestic production of raw wool, while the manufactories within their borders required 55.97 per cent. of the entire amount of domestic wool used as raw material in the United States.   If to the New England states are added New York, New Jersey and Pennsylvania, the combined percentage of consumption in manufactories was 85.21, while that of production was but 9.64.   The manufactories north of the Ohio and Potomac rivers

and east of the Mississippi river required 92.77 per cent.
of the domestic wool used as raw material, though they
produced but 34.88 per cent. of the total wool clip. The
entire consumption of raw wool by manufactories out-
side of this territory was not as great a percentage
of the total as was the production of the single
state of California of the aggregate domestic production. The states separately contributing as
much as 5 per cent. of the wool clip of 1890 were
Ohio, Michigan, Texas, Montana, Utah, Oregon
and California, their aggregate production being
56.31 per cent. of the total for the country, against
which their percentage of consumption in manufactures was but 4.45.   Practically, therefore, the entire
production of raw wool has to be transported from the
sheep raising regions west of the Allegheny Mountains
to the states adjacent to the Atlantic seaboard and
north of Chesapeake bay.   After this has been accomplished, and the raw material has been converted into
clothing or other woolen products, transportation facilities are again required to distribute the finished goods
among those by whom they are to be consumed, including in many instances the residents of the very regions
from which the raw materials were originally shipped.
The concentration of agricultural industry is especially
remarkable when it is borne in mind that all are
dependent upon its results. Twenty-five states, or about
one-half of the total, produce 98 per cent. of the cotton,
95 per cent. of the corn, 95 per cent. of the barley, 93
per cent. of the oats and from eight-tenths to nine-tenths
of the wheat, rye, buckwheat, tobacco, potatoes and hay
produced in the entire country.   The concentration in

particular localities of the business of manufacturing boots and shoes and paper, of refining sugar, of raising and of slaughtering cattle for food are all evidences of the operation of the same tendencies, and whatever benefits have resulted can be shown to have been dependent upon cheap transportation. As the term cheap transportation, except when applied to movement between points connected by natural or artificial waterways, is synonymous with railway transportation, it is clear that whatever socially profitable consequences have accrued from the process illustrated are attributable to railway development.

CHAPTER XII.

SOCIALLY PROFITABLE TRANSPORTATION.

Two extreme social conditions in regard to transportation are conceivable and may aid in determining in what extent it is economically desirable that individuals and commodities should move from community to community. First, a very crude state of society, in which each community produces everything which it consumes, and is consequently economically independent. Under such conditions the standard of living is limited by local productive resources, and the difficulty with which the indispensable means of subsistence are procured under frequently unfavorable conditions of soil and climate, confines population to certain localities, preventing the settlement of many regions the resources of which, though bountiful in regard to particular commodities, are not sufficiently diverse to permit the production of all of the necessaries of life. These circumstances, as well as the limit imposed upon possible aggregate production, effectually retard the natural growth of population. The second conception is of a society, at the other end of the developmental process, in which each community has been connected with every other community by adequate transportation facilities, the maintenance and operation of which have been provided for by a system of general taxation, and the use of the facilities placed, free of charge, at the disposal of everyone who cares to make use of them. A country subject to such conditions would, as their ultimate result, be divided into regions of varying areas, each of which could produce a single commodity within a maximum cost established by the cost of the last increment of the supply demanded by the whole country, and the industry of each of these regions would be expended in the production of the single commodity so indicated. Evidently the social conditions involved in neither of these conceptions are desirable. In the one case cost of production would be higher than were exchanges of products between different communities possible, while in the other the cost of production would be enhanced by the disregard of the variations in cost of different transportation services. It is possible that this point requires elucidation. For any particular society and at any definite time, under whatever system of production may be in vogue, the complex of articles required for consumption has a certain, though possibly not an ascertainable, cost of production. The amount of transportation involved in the system of production in use in such a country can be increased, or, assuming that some transportation is used, it can be diminished. Either course will be desirable if it will result in reducing the total cost of production. The diagram on opposite page will, it is hoped, assist in making clear the point advanced.

For the purposes of this discussion let it be assumed that the outer circle is the boundary of a country which is, economically, entirely isolated and independent, and that the inner circle contains a community (A) composed entirely of individuals not directly engaged in production, such as lawyers, bankers, railway presidents, ministers, teachers, etc., and includes all such non-producers in the country. Then, if the other inhabitants of

the country desire the services of the residents of A, the
former will have to supply the latter with subsistence.
Let it be assumed that each of the regions between different pairs of circles is capable of producing subsistence
for the entire population of the country; that for the producers with equal expenditures of energy, but when

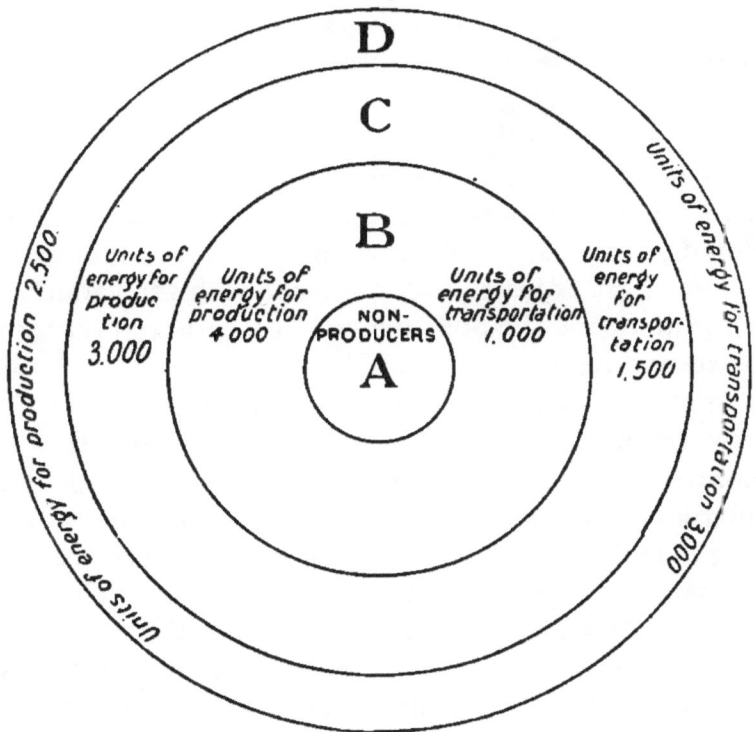

called upon to furnish a surplus sufficient to supply the
requirements of the non-producers in A, the varying resources make varying expenditures of energy necessary.
Suppose that for the production of the surplus necessary to supply A with subsistence the expenditure requi-

site in B amounts to 4000 units of energy, in C to 3000, and in D to 2500, and that the number of units of energy required to transport this surplus from B to A is 1000, from C to A 1500, and from D to A 3000. The relative advantages of utilizing each of the three productive regions would then be as indicated below:

SOCIAL COST.

If production is in region:—	Number of units of energy required —		
	For local production.	For transportation.	Total.
B	4,000	1,000	5,000
C	3,000	1,500	4,500
D	2,500	3,000	5,500

Evidently under these conditions it would be most profitable for the society in question to cultivate the region C, which it would certainly do if transportation charges were adjusted in accordance with the variations in the amounts of labor involved in transportation from the several regions. It should be observed that it is not alleged that these variations in the expenditures of energy requisite for different services correspond with those in distance. It is desired merely to affirm that different transportation services do involve different aggregates of energy, and that these differences are important in connection with the adjustment of charges. If, in the case assumed, these differences should be disregarded by making equal transportation rates for all services, production would be carried on in region D, though at a loss of 1000 units of energy. If, on the other hand, rates were so high that energy expended in transportation was over-remunerated, the result might be to confine production to region B at a social loss of the advantage that might have been gained by cultivating C. Suppose, for instance, that the compensation for a unit of energy expended in moving commodities was three times that for one expended in local production. Then only the tract B would be cultivated. Similarly too low charges might relegate production to region D. From this analysis it appears to be socially desirable that energy expended in the business of transportation shall receive the same remuneration as a similar amount of energy expended in other lines of production, and that rates for different transportation services shall vary in accordance with the different amounts of energy required to perform them in order that society shall have neither too much nor too little transportation. It is believed that in the United States, at the present time and under current conditions, there is quite as much danger of too low as of too high rates for railway services, and that in some sections there has been much transportation that was socially undesirable because it actually enhanced the real cost of production.

Readers have no doubt observed that no attempt has been made to apply the principles developed to the rates for moving specific commodities or for any particular services. The facts which make such an application impracticable, as well as the real utility of these principles, will be discussed in another chapter.

CHAPTER XIII.

HOW SOCIALLY UNDESIRABLE TRANSPORTATION MAY OCCUR.

Having in the preceding chapter established the principle that there can be so much transportation as actually to increase the expenditure of social energy in production, it will be useful to discover in what manner an industrial system in which the element of transportation is unduly prominent may arise. It is obvious that the aggregate amount of transportation can be augmented by an absolute increase in the number of tons carried, or by an increase in the average distance traversed by each ton. Though the demand for most commodities increases as the price decreases, and the latter is usually determined by the cost of production, including transportation charges to the point of consumption, demand cannot be increased indefinitely and the rate of increase is generally diminished by each successive increment until the point is reached beyond which demand cannot go, because the desires of consumers are completely satisfied.

At whatever prices may prevail the demand in any market at a definite point of time for each of the articles which constitute the complex of commodities required for the subsistence of the community dependent upon that market establishes the quantity of each article which will be accepted. Consumers are, however, quite indifferent as to the proportions in which the sums paid by them for subsistence are distributed between those who produce, respectively, what have been termed, form utilities and place utilities. Consequently while extensive reductions in prices are usually necessary in order considerably to augment the quantity of goods for which there is an effective demand it is quite possible with but insignificant reductions in prices caused by very slight decreases in the rates for moving goods to multiply the aggregate of transportation. Suppose that during a definite period the city of New York requires for consumption and export 25,000 tons of wheat for which it will pay $30 per ton, and that the supply must be obtained from the regions given in the following table, which also gives certain assumed costs of production in each, and of transportation from each to New York:

Region.	Distance from New York in miles.	Tons supplied.	Cost of production per ton.*	Freight rates to New York per ton.	Total cost of production at New York per ton.
A	200	7,000	$25.00	$4.00	$29.00
B	400	6,000	24.00	5.25	29.25
C	700	5,000	23.00	6.50	29.50
D	1,100	4,000	22.00	7.75	29.75
E	1,600	3,000	21.00	9.00	30.00
F	2,200	None.	19.00	12.00	31.00

*Of form utilities only.

Obviously such a condition could not exist unless regions A, B, C and D were so cultivated as to produce all the wheat which could be marketed in New York from each respective region without the cost of production rising above $30 per ton, but it is quite reasonable to suppose, and will be assumed, for the purposes of the present discussion, that the productions of regions E and F are susceptible of considerable increase. Under the conditions shown in the table the total transportation of wheat for the New York market, during the

period in question, would be equivalent to carrying 16,-
500,000 tons one mile.   Whenever such a condition exists, however, there are certain to be many persons who,
attracted by the natural resources of region F, will seek
to secure rates for transportation from that region to
New York which will permit them to produce wheat in
F for the market in New York.   Suppose they secure
a reduction of one dollar per ton from the rate from F
shown in the table.   Producers in F will then be on an
equality with those in E in the common market, and it
may be assumed that they will be able to sell half of the
total quantity required from the two regions which have
the marginal cost of production.   If so, the aggregate
transportation performed in getting wheat to the New
York market becomes equivalent to 17,400,000 ton-miles
without any decrease in the price at New York. Producers at E will not see their business lost without a struggle, and may in time secure a reduction in transportation charges on their production, say, to $8.10 per ton,
which will enable them to market their wheat in New
York at $29.10 per ton.   If E can produce all but 7000
tons of the quantity which New York will purchase at
the latter price, and this amount will of course be somewhat larger than at $30, the former price, the price will
be reduced to the figure thus established, and production for the New York market will be confined to regions A and E, while the total transportation will have
been increased to more than 22,200,000 ton-miles.   Society will then have the advantage of cheaper wheat
against which to offset the disadvantage, apparent at
least, of having to perform more transportation in order
to get it, and of having regions B, C, D and F aban-

doned as far as the industry of producing wheat is concerned. The balance of social gain or loss must be determined, if at all, in accordance with the general principle, advanced in the twelfth chapter.

Supposing the conditions indicated in the table to exist, there is another way in which they might be modified, which does not seem radically dissimilar from some of the legislative attempts at railway regulation that have occasionally received energetic and noisy advocacy. Legislation may require that all of the rates in force be reduced one-half. If this is done, region F can market wheat in New York at $25 per ton; E at $25.50; D at $25.88; C at $26.25; B at $26.63, and A at $27.

Under the circumstances the price cannot go above $27 unless more wheat is demanded than can be produced in the six regions named. If F can produce all that is wanted, the price will be $25, and considerably more wheat will be taken than at $30, but the transportation performed in moving the 25,000 tons formerly · demanded will have been increased to the equivalent of moving 55,000,000 tons one mile. If the productions of both E and F are required to meet the effective demand, the price in New York will be $25.50, somewhat less wheat will be consumed than at $25 per ton, and there will be a smaller aggregate transportation. In either case the cultivation of wheat in the intermediate regions will have been abandoned. The slightest familiarity with the history of the agricultural industry in the United States will show that such changes in transportation charges have produced exactly such results and have, in many instances, caused the abandonment of once profitable farms and the transfer of food production to more remote regions.   Doubtless in some instances the social consequences have been good, in others ill.   The balance is favorable if wants are satisfied with a smaller expenditure, unfavorable if with a greater expenditure of energy than would have been required had the former adjustment been maintained.

CHAPTER XIV.

SHOULD THE BUSINESS OF RAILWAY TRANSPORTATION BE REMUNERATIVE?

Railway problems are frequently discussed as though there existed a distinct line of demarkation between the interests of the general public, which is assumed for the purpose to consist wholly of purchasers of transportation, and the interests of those by whom it is furnished. That this view is superficial is already evident to those who have seen that too cheap transportation inevitably results in too much transportation. They are aware that the general public not only purchases, but also supplies railway transportation, and that if the energy expended in the production of place utilities, that is, in moving commodities to the localities in which they will be most useful, receives relatively lower compensation than that expended in the production of form utilities, an undesirably large aggregate amount of transportation will be demanded in pursuance of the desire of consumers to obtain supplies at the lowest practicable money cost, and so large an amount of energy will be diverted from the latter to the former kind of production that the average return per unit of energy expended in production of all kinds will be materially reduced.

The compensation for energy expended in those forms of industry in which there is free competition is so regulated thereby that when the returns from one industry fall below the general level, energy is gradually diverted therefrom until the lessening of the supply produces an increase in the price of the commodity furnished

or the service rendered which restores the equilibrium.
That the opposite effect can be produced in the railway
industry is attributable to the fact that capital in the
form of railway facilities cannot be withdrawn and applied to other purposes than those of transportation,
supplemented, as it unquestionably is in the United
States, by the further fact that in many sections of the
country railway construction has been artificially stimulated, until the means of land transportation are actually
in excess not only of present requirements, but also of
any that may reasonably be anticipated in the near
future. When the owners of a particular railway find
themselves in a situation in which it is impossible to
secure a return upon their capital equal to that currently
paid to other forms of capital in the same community,
they cannot transfer their investments to other industries, but must continue to operate the facilities in existence or abandon them entirely. The choice is between
a loss of the entire capital or the acceptance of a return
so small that, if continued without increase, it amounts
to the loss of a portion of the original investment. Naturally capitalists so situated accept the lesser evil and
continue to operate the property as long as traffic sufficient to pay the actual expenses of operation and the
smallest return to investors can be secured. Mobility
of capital among many industries is effected without the
actual withdrawal of investments, through the refusal
of capitalists to furnish means for ordinary repairs and
renewals and for the development of particular industries in proportion to the growing demands of an increasing population, unless their investments are adequately rewarded. Lacking these checks, it is possible,

in communities which afe industrially retrograding or stagnant, for the remuneration accorded to the energy expended in railway transportation to be progressively reduced until only that portion which is in the form of current labor is adequately compensated. When this occurs the processes of production become in a social sense unnecessarily costly.

The railways of the United States give employment to about 800,000 men, who receive as wages more than 60 per cent. of their annual gross earnings. There are dependent upon railway employes not less than 3,000,000 women and children, so that there must be nearly four millions of individuals, or about one in every seventeen of the entire population whose livelihoods come directly from the business of moving passengers and property by rail. It would be difficult to estimate the number of those who produce the necessaries and luxuries demanded by railway employes and their families, or who perform other services in their behalf; yet it is unquestionable that any circumstances which should materially reduce the number or the earning capacity of the latter would seriously restrict the market in which millions of industrious individuals dispose of their products and services. In order, therefore, that the adjustment between different occupations be not needlessly destroyed, measures having for their object the reduction of railway earnings should be carefully scrutinized.

Though there are doubtless portions of the United States in which railway construction has been so extravagantly conducted as to be in excess of the probable requirements for many years to come, there are other regions which are inadequately served. The develop-

ment of these regions requires the creation of railway
facilities, but for the last few years, at least, the capital
necessary has not been readily available. The explanation is not hard to find. Those who examine the opportunities for new railway enterprises naturally study
the results of previous investments, and, finding many
unprofitable railways, are told that this condition is attributable to over-taxation, unjust legislation, and,
above all, to the legal necessity of maintaining a burden-
some and wasteful competitive system of operation.
They learn also that in many communities, including
some of those in which new railways are most needed,
the attitude of prominent politicians and influential legislators is distinctly antagonistic to the owners and managers of railway properties. From the standpoint of
the capitalist who is considering the advisability of in-
vesting in a new railway enterprise, these conditions
simply add a new element of risk to those which would
naturally attend such an investment. Business operations approach the limit of mere gambling transactions
as one extreme when the risk involved is great, and as
it diminishes approach the other extreme, in which it is
almost absent, of loaning money on ample security.
Though capitalists can usually be found who will accept
quite hazardous risks, they invariably demand opportunities for such considerable gains as seem to them commensurate with the chances of loss. Those who undertake railway construction under the conditions described insist, therefore, upon an at least speculative
opportunity to obtain compensation for the extraordinary risk imposed by a condition of public sentiment
which may eventuate in legislative attacks upon the

property created. Society has found it expedient to delegate to groups of individuals, termed corporations, the business of furnishing and operating railway facilities, and it would seem that it should be willing to allow those who accept the task reasonable remuneration for the sacrifices involved. A growing community must do so, or it cannot readily obtain adequate facilities for railway transportation; one already amply provided in that respect must do so, or there will be an excessive and unprofitable use of the transportation facilities already in existence.

CHAPTER XV.

ENERGY EXPENDED ON JOINT ACCOUNT.

If it were possible to apply the principle which has formed the basis of the discussion in the last three chapters of this work to the charge exacted for each specific transportation service performed by a railway, one of the most difficult of railway problems would be much nearer than it is to a satisfactory solution. Unfortunately this cannot be done, for much of the energy expended in railway transportation is applied without reference to the movement of any particular traffic. When society, through its ordinary processes, determines to employ a portion of its available resources in the construction of an improved highway, the advantages to be gained by increasing the mobility of all of the persons and property for which the new route is available form the controlling consideration and energy is expended in behalf of the aggregate traffic which is anticipated, and not of any mere portion thereof. The telegraph facilities maintained by every railway are not provided in order that either passengers or freight alone may be satisfactorily moved, but, rather, to insure the safe and rapid transportation of both. Similarly, the coal consumed by the locomotive of a passenger train is not mined, brought to the railway terminal, loaded upon the tender and consumed in the fire-box for the exclusive benefit either of local or of through traffic. It is not sufficient to assert the impracticability of assigning these expenditures of energy, or definite portions thereof, to particular services for which they have been

incurred, for it should be clearly understood, not only
that this cannot be accomplished, but that the expenditure of none of these unassignable portions of the energy
devoted to railway transportation is made in behalf of a
specific item or items in the aggregate traffic.   This
will be clearly understood by assuming the existence of
a railway which is engaged exclusively in carrying an
unchanging quantity of a single commodity in but one
direction between its terminals only.   It would be practicable, with regard to such a road, to divide the entire
energy expended in construction, equipment, maintenance and operation among the units of traffic; but if in
the progress of time it should become possible for the
railway to obtain a return load for its cars, it is apparent
that the additional energy which would have to be expended would be very slight.   The new traffic would
have to be loaded into the cars which were formerly
returned empty and removed therefrom when it had
reached its destination, but there would be little additional wear of roadbed or equipment and only slightly
greater consumption of coal.   If charges on the new
traffic were to be based upon the additional energy
expended in order to carry it, they would be very slight
indeed, while, on the other hand, if they were made
proportional to the charges exacted on the traffic formerly transported the total remuneration received by
the railway would be too high.   The problem, which is
mainly a theoretical one, seems to have been solved
in the minds of most individuals in favor of a reduction
in the charges for the service formerly performed, so
that each shall share in compensating the energy which,
though indispensable to both, is directly incurred for
neither.

In practice the traffic of railways consists of a great many different commodities, some of which are carried in all directions and between a very large number of points. With regard to each specific service, it is usually possible to ascertain just what energy would not have been called for had it not been performed; but the total so assignable is insignificant when compared with that which cannot be distributed. All that can then be accomplished by the application of the principle outlined in the twelfth chapter to the practical operations of railways is to insure the just remuneration, in the aggregate, of the energy expended in railway transportation,—*i.e.*, that the total revenue derived from all traffic is neither more nor less than the amount necessary to compensate each unit of energy equally with units of energy expended in the production of form utilities. The principle cannot be applied to the relations among charges for different services, and every attempt to do so is necessarily unscientific and dangerous.

It has already been shown that the conditions to which the railway industry is subject make it practically certain that the total revenues collected will not be excessive, and it is equally certain that the enlightened self-interest of those engaged in the business will not permit the total recompense to the capital or labor involved permanently to fall below what is reasonable and just. Society, therefore, in order to protect itself against too much and too little transportation, has only to see that the business of the carriers is conducted by those to whom its management has been committed without the latter being hampered by legislative or customary restrictions involving wasteful expenditures, and that the speculative element is eliminated, as far as practicable, from railway investments.

That the total revenue should reasonably compensate those whose capital or labor is required for the conduct of the railway business is sufficiently evident, but how is the burden of furnishing this revenue to be distributed among the purchasers of railway transportation considered as individuals, as constituting communities or as producers or consumers of special commodities or classes of goods? What proportions, for instance, of the aggregate revenue necessary to recompense the services performed by the railways of the United States may reasonably be collected respectively from passengers, from wheat, from cotton, from manufactured products, from persons living west of the Mississippi river, from the Standard Oil Company, or from John Doe? Of the various answers which have been given none has been in any degree satisfactory, and it has long been regarded by students as practically impossible to elaborate any principle or set of principles which will definitely and clearly meet the various requirements of the almost innumerable problems which may arise in the adjustment of the relations among the charges for different transportation services. These problems are among the most difficult of those which demand the attention of railway managers in the administration of the properties in their charge, and to the constant and seemingly inevitable recourse to methods of solution determined by expediency rather than by principle, may not unjustly be attributed much of the popular discontent which has resulted in harsh and unjust railway legislation.

CHAPTER XVI.

RELATIVELY REASONABLE RATES.

The aggregate sum which may reasonably be exacted for railway services having been ascertained in accordance with the principles already indicated, it becomes necessary to determine upon the respective amounts or proportions of that aggregate which should be contributed thereto by those for whom specific transportation services are performed. As the variations in the aggregate revenue which is necessary reasonably to compensate the energy devoted to the railway business that are caused by the addition to or subtraction from the total representing all of the services performed of single items are usually so small as to be practically negligible, it is clearly impossible to predicate of any particular charge that it is, considered alone, either reasonable or unreasonable, extortionate or unduly low. It follows that whether a particular charge is just or unjust must be determined by considering its relation to charges for other services, and that of the revenue which it brings to the railway corporation to the total revenue required for the maintenance and operation of its property and the just compensation of those who have furnished its capital in the light of the circumstances and conditions governing the service for which it was exacted. When a railway makes different charges for carrying different articles, for moving different quantities of the same article, or for moving the same article between different stations, it is properly said to discriminate among the respective services rendered. Such discriminations may be reasonable and just, or they may be unreasonable and unjust. They are the former if they accurately measure substantial differences in the circumstances and conditions attending the different services, and the latter if they arbitrarily disregard such circumstances and conditions. Nothing could be more unjust or socially detrimental than the exaction of equal charges for all transportation services. Such rates would have to be fixed so low as to produce insufficient revenue and to result consequently in the performance of more transportation than is desirable, or they would be practically prohibitive of many territorial exchanges of articles the value of which is comparatively low in proportion to their weight and bulk. On the other hand, arbitrary and unfair discriminations in the charges for railway services are seriously detrimental. If they unduly favor particular individuals at the expense of their commercial rivals, they are incompatible with equality of individual opportunity; tend to make the friendly patronage of railway officials a more important factor in commercial success than intelligence, industry or integrity, and finally to produce those immense industrial combinations which, whatever may be said of them in general, when founded upon artificial conditions, constitute a very menacing characteristic of the current industrial system. If they give unjust advantage to traffic in particular commodities, they favor unfairly the producers and consumers of those commodities, furnish, in many cases, an incentive to those who are willing to resort to adulteration or substitution, and often compel the extensive use of inferior and less desirable articles which can be made, though unsatisfactorily, to serve the same purposes. If they unfairly favor particular localities, such regions are given a monopoly privilege, and industry may be diverted to them from regions naturally better adapted to the particular kind of production involved. The development of industry is thus unnaturally stimulated in one region, while at the same time it is, in another, artificially retarded, thus producing an unsymmetrical organization, which cannot fail to enhance the difficulty of producing the aggregate subsistence required by society. It may be taken for granted, therefore, that just discriminations in the charges exacted for railway services cannot be based upon the individuals for whom those services are performed, whether considered separately, as constituting industrial or social groups, as members of communities, or as producers or consumers of particular commodities. Such reasonable discriminations will not afford advantages to particular individuals on account of their professional, political, social or commercial standing, the character of the businesses in which they are engaged, the extent or number of their commercial transactions, or, what is almost the same thing, the quantity of transportation which they purchase (except as the latter circumstance constitutes a condition which substantially affects the service rendered by the railway), nor unduly on account of the place of their residence or the location of their farms, factories, warehouses or stores. Relatively just rates will not place a locality at a commercial disadvantage on account of the number of its inhabitants, the degree of their geographical concentration, or their political affiliations, nor on account of its economic organization, the character of its productive resources, or the number, extent or financial condition of the railway lines by which it is served.

On the other hand, it is perfectly legitimate for railway officials to base discriminations in charges upon every substantial difference in the circumstances and conditions which affect or control the performance of each specific service, and the economic interests of society share with the narrower pecuniary interests of those engaged directly in the business of railway transportation the benefits which result from such discriminations when they are intelligently based upon a comprehensive knowledge of actual conditions and a keen appreciation of their ultimate consequences. Primarily, it is desirable that existing railway facilities should be utilized to their fullest profitable capacity. Society should not be compelled to continue the production of form utilities with difficulty and under unfavorable local conditions when the same articles might be made available to consumers in the same locality with a lower aggregate expenditure of energy by diverting a part of that employed in producing form utilities to the production of place utilities. Society is forced to accept this unnecessary sacrifice of productive energy whenever a railway refuses or is compelled to refuse any increment of traffic because, though it could be made to pay an amount sufficient to compensate the increment of the total expenditure of energy which it actually causes, it cannot be made to contribute what is considered its just proportion of fixed charges. Whatever disadvantages may appertain to that view of railway business which so subordinates its public nature as to permit those who hold it to urge that only those considerations which govern the vendors of ordinary commodities in fixing their prices, or those who perform ordinary services in charging therefor, should be allowed to control in the adjustment of railway charges, it has the great advantage that the functions of the railways as carriers are not likely to be limited by any artificial restrictions compelling the rejection of traffic which could be moved with profit to the carriers and with beneficial economic results to the community.

The nearest approximation to a general rule regarding the adjustment of railway charges which it seems safe to base upon the present knowledge of the relations of the transportation business to industry in general is that an adjustment of rates is desirable under which sufficient revenue will be secured from each particular item of traffic justly to remunerate those expenditures of energy which would not have been incurred had not the particular services involved been performed, and which without preventing the movement of any traffic from which this minimum of revenue can be continuously obtained will, in the long run, secure in addition from each item the largest practicable contribution toward reasonable remuneration of those expenditures of energy which are incurred on joint account.

CHAPTER XVII.

UNJUST DISCRIMINATION IN GENERAL.

Though it is perfectly clear that the relative advantages and disadvantages resulting from unjust discriminations in railway charges must accrue to the benefit or detriment of individuals or groups of individuals, such discriminations may be classified with regard to their incidence as being in favor of (a) particular purchasers of transportation selected from among the residents of the same region, (b) all of the members of particular communities, or (c) all of those interested in the movement of particular commodities or classes of traffic. There is a second classification of considerable utility, founded upon the manner in which unjust discriminations are effected, whether (a) by means of deviations from a reasonable adjustment provided for in the regular published schedules of charges or (b) by means of the establishment of relatively unreasonable rates which are promulgated in the tariffs and classifications of freight. These classifications coincide in some degree for discriminations which are intended unjustly to favor particular purchasers of transportation to the disadvantage of competitors in the same locality, from whom higher charges are exacted for identical and contemporaneous services, are necessarily effected by means of deviations from the schedules of charges regularly made public. Such deviations may be accomplished by the payment of rebates to favored patrons, by accepting shipments at weights that are known to be understated, by permitting traffic to be charged for as though moved a shorter distance than that actually traversed, by excessive allowances for terminal or other services performed by shippers or consignees, by excessive payments for mileage of shippers' cars, and by many other devices, all of which, when practiced by railways in connection with the movement of interstate commerce, are prohibited by the Interstate Commerce law, and render those who perpetrate and those who accept them liable upon detection to punishment by fine and imprisonment. As it is unquestionably unjust to charge differently for identical services performed for different patrons proof of any of the practices enumerated is conclusive evidence of unjust discrimination, and it is quite proper and practicable to apply the penalties considered suitable for such discriminations to the acts by which they are effected. On the other hand, it is reasonable and just that different rates should be applied to the movement of the same commodity between different points, or to that of different commodities between the same points; and the existence of such discriminations is by no means evidence of injustice. In order to prove the existence of the latter it is necessary to show that the difference in charges is greater or less than that warranted by the difference in the circumstances and conditions attending the performance of the respective services. Similarly, the existence of a relatively unfair adjustment of charges can be demonstrated by showing that substantially different services are performed under similar circumstances for equal compensation, though an examination of the schedules of charges would not only fail to show an unjust discrimination, but would apparently preclude the existence of any discrimination whatever.

The inquiries necessary in order to establish the fact that the relations among charges for different services place at an unjust disadvantage the residents of a particular locality, or the producers of a particular commodity are therefore quite extensive and intricate. Such unreasonable discriminations may even result from errors of judgment on the part of those having rate-making authority, and it would be manifestly a misuse of legislative power to apply to them penalties as severe as those attached to practices which cannot be resorted to except in pursuance of a deliberate intention to afford unfair advantage to a particular patron or patrons. An award of damages equivalent to the injury sustained, though by no means an entirely satisfactory means of redress, and the correction of the charges so as to make them relatively reasonable in future, appears to be all the relief which legislatures should venture to apply.

It is important to observe that no railway can discriminate unjustly among its patrons without injury to itself, for in interfering arbitrarily with the natural organization of industry it introduces artificial conditions which cannot fail ultimately to retard the commercial development of the region which it serves, and that this fact is so thoroughly realized by most railway managers that the unreasonable rate purposely and voluntarily made by a railway official is exceedingly rare. Such rates are almost invariably expedients adopted in the face of exigencies in which the sacrifice of valuable traffic appears to be the alternative. There seems but little popular appreciation of the extent in which railways are, under current conditions, subject to the dictation of those who ship in large quantities and of large combinations

of shippers. As long as the relations among railways
are such that the corporation owning a particular
line can obtain an at least temporary pecuniary
profit by diverting traffic from another line, those who
are able to control shipments, the revenue from which is
of considerable importance, by threatening to take all
of their traffic from the line whose rate-making officer obstinately refuses to.favor them unjustly, and to
bestow upon it a line served by one more complacent,
will be able to secure concessions which will place other
shippers at a distinct disadvantage. By this means a
single shipper or a group of shippers whose combined
business operations are of large extent may be able to
obtain unfair advantage over competitors doing business in the same locality, or the entire traffic of a large
city may be favored as against that of adjacent towns,
or the shipments of an industrial group may be preferred above those of other groups. The demand for
the concession desired may be made directly and unre-
servedly by the officer of a manufacturing corporation
or trust, it may take the form of a representation insist-
ing upon the obligation of a particular railway to maintain the interests of a city with which its historical or
financial relations are intimate and peculiar, or public
sentiment or legislative enactment may demand that a
particular industry be made artificially profitable by
charging some part of the cost of transportation which
it should bear upon others which are naturally remunerative.

CHAPTER XVIII.

UNJUST DISCRIMINATION AMONG INDIVIDUALS.

Though it was found convenient at a very early period in the development of railway transportation to print schedules of the charges in force for the numerous services which such carriers were ready to perform, railway officials did not consider themselves bound by the rates named in these schedules, and lower charges were very frequently, if not invariably, granted for shipments between points connected by two or more routes to those whose traffic was important in quantity. Prior to the enactment of the Interstate Commerce law, in 1887, there appears to have been, at least so far as traffic passing state or territorial lines was concerned, no legal obligation to treat different patrons equally, for, though at Common Law no carrier could exact more than a reasonable sum for its services, the courts do not appear to have recognized the interdependence of railway rates, and it was not considered illegal to collect less than a reasonable rate from one patron while exacting the full maximum which justice, or what was thus considered to be justice, would permit from another patron for an identical and contemporaneous service. Under such circumstances only unsophisticated shippers, or those whose traffic had but the slightest importance to the railways, paid the rates between competitive points named in the printed schedules; and even at points served by single carriers concessions from the printed charges were by no means uncommon. It was customary for a prospective shipper to secure offers from the agents of all of the rival lines, and, according to an official statement made by Mr. C. C. McCain, probably the highest authority on the history of railway charges in the United States, the instances prior to 1887 in which the full published rates were charged were exceptional, and deviations therefrom were the rule.

The requirement that charges for like and contemporaneous services should be equal though such services were performed for different individuals, which was made a basic portion of the Interstate Commerce law, was as revolutionary as it is just and salutary. Had the observance of this provision been secured one of the principal evils which have accompanied the administration of railway properties would have been corrected, but unfortunately Congress not only failed to provide adequately for its enforcement, but in the same law which forbade unjust discriminations prohibited those measures which, when voluntarily adopted by competing railways, had been the most effective in preventing such discriminations. Discrimination among individuals constitutes the ordinary weapon of competitive warfare among parallel routes. In consequence of modern specialization of productive functions the larger commercial interests at what are called competitive points are usually concentrated in a few lines of production. Considerations relating to the convenience of the carriers as well as to that of their patrons usually impel the former to provide especially for handling and transporting the traffic supplied by such interests, and this, together with the magnitude of the business they furnish, renders it the particular object of whatever competition may occur. Under ordinary circumstances competition among sellers finds expression in a series of offers to supply the particular commodity vended at varying prices, this series of offers finally resulting in a practically uniform price which approximates the cost of production of the marginal increment of the supply for which there is an effective demand. Such offers are open to all, and do not vary in regard to the individual to whom they are made. Among railways such is not the ordinary course of competition. Particular transportation services having no definite and ascertainable cost of production to serve as a natural limit to competition, open offers would ultimately result in uniform, though unreasonably and ruinously low charges, and traffic would seek the lines naturally best adapted to carry each particular shipment. Each line attempts therefore to keep secret its concessions to shippers, and in order to do so makes them to particular patrons only. Hence arise unjust discriminations, upon which are built up extortionate profits and finally enormous industrial combinations, which in time are able effectively to demand favors in the adjustment of railway charges and to dictate the terms upon which they will purchase transportation. No one has better expressed these facts than Hon. Martin A. Knapp, the present chairman of the Interstate Commerce Commission. In the course of one of the most satisfactory papers on railway problems ever written, he said:

"* * the choice lies between competition on the one hand, with the inevitable outcome of discriminations which favor the few at the expense of the many, or like charges for like service, which can be realized only by permitting and encouraging co-operative action by rival railroads. *The power to compete is the power to discriminate*, and it is simply out of the question to have at once the absence of discrimination and the presence of competition."

And in the same article:

> "The ultimate effect of preferential rates is to concentrate the commerce of the country in a few hands. The favored shipper, who is usually the large shipper, is furnished with a weapon against which skill, energy and experience are alike unavailing. When the natural advantages of capital are augmented by exemptions from charges commonly imposed it becomes powerful enough to force all rivals from the field. If we could unearth the secrets of those modern 'trusts,' whose surprising exploits excite such wide apprehension, we should find an explanation- of their menacing growth in the systematic methods by which they have evaded the burdens of transportation. The reduced charges which they have obtained, sometimes by favoritism and oftener by force, account in great measure for the colossal gains which they have accumulated. This is the sleight of hand by which the marvel has been produced, the key to the riddle which has amazed and alarmed the nation. If these combinations were deprived of their special and exclusive rates there is little doubt that they would be shorn of their greatest strength and lose their dangerous supremacy. Indeed, I think it scarcely too much to say that no alliance of capital, no aggregation of productive forces would prove of real or at least of permanent disadvantage if rigidly subjected to just and impartial charges for public transportation."

No one believes that the evil of unjust discrimination has been materially mitigated by the Interstate Commerce law. The requirements of the law furnish a ready reply to the applicant for a reduced rate who cannot turn his request into an effective demand by demonstrating his ability to divert important traffic to another line. The shipper of unimportant traffic no longer "shops" among rival lines, and it may usually be taken for granted that he pays the full published rates. Whatever concessions are made are granted grudgingly and reluctantly to the few shippers whose favor the railways cannot lose without sacrificing important revenue; but as long as such concessions continue to be made the fact that they are restricted to a favored and powerful few aggravates their detrimental results. Thus it appears that the Interstate Commerce law, which could by no means perpetuate competition among railways and at the same time abolish the ordinary means by which it is conducted, has conferred upon the favored shippers this inestimable boon—they can feel reasonably sure that the illegal favors which they enjoy are not granted to those who ship in smaller quantities.

CHAPTER XIX.

UNJUST DISCRIMINATION AMONG PLACES.

If the published rates from different producing regions to a common market are relatively reasonable and just, but certain shippers doing business in one of those regions are given more favorable rates than those in the printed schedules which are observed with reference to both their local and non-local competitors, the injustice by which they profit will enable them to draw to the community in which they reside a larger portion of the business of supplying the common market than it would otherwise enjoy. Local competitors may be driven from business and the gains which accrue from the increased trade may be monopolized in greater or less extent by the minority in the community who have been especially favored in transportation charges; but notwithstanding these drawbacks, the community, considered for the time being as an economic unit, will have been given a distinct advantage in rates over competing communities. It is not necessary here to consider whether the unfair distribution within the community apparently favored is so far incompatible with the highest utilization of its available productive energy as to offset the unjust advantage in rates, for it is the present purpose merely to show that secret concessions to preferred shippers may amount to unjust discriminations in favor of the localities in which they do business.

Though the foregoing is a not uncommon type of territorial discrimination, that which may be considered characteristic is not the result of secret deviations from fair rates, but of unfair charges openly promulgated. These are usually the result of competition among railways offering to perform identical services, and the unfairness, having its origin in circumstances for which the railways are in no way responsible, is attributable to the public sentiment which has permitted the enactment and continuance of legislation which interferes with the mitigation of those circumstances and the reasonable limitation of the competition in which they result rather than to any dereliction on the part of railway owners or managers. The advantage in the adjustment of railway charges enjoyed by the locality served by several railways over that served by but one is so completely recognized by the general public, which however does not usually perceive that it is the consequence of unjust discrimination, that it has proved a considerable incentive to the construction of unnecessary and therefore socially wasteful parallel lines. Competition at terminal points impels most railways to charge relatively high rates at intermediate points, the traffic of which cannot be diverted to other lines and at stations on branch lines which are not served by other carriers. Such discriminations tend artificially to stimulate the concentration of production in the favored localities and may so effectively counteract the possibly superior natural resources enjoyed by the regions which they subject to unjust disadvantage as to divert the industry affected from the region in which it could be conducted with the least expenditure of effort.

If a particular community competes with others for the privilege of supplying a common market, and through an unfair adjustment of transportation charges secures

an advantage amounting to an injustice to the others,
it is quite evident that it is of no consequence to the
latter or to society, which is ultimately compelled to
produce the commodity involved with unnecessary difficulty or to use less satisfactory substitutes, whether the
injustice is the result of the action of a single railway or
of several. A case decided by the Interstate Commerce
Commission during 1892 affords an interesting illustration of an adjustment of rates for which, though it
was resulting in the commercial destruction and de-
population of a formerly thriving town, no single railway could be held fully responsible. The Board of
Trade of Eau Claire, Wisconsin, claimed that the
charges exacted for moving the lumber produced in the
mills of that city to the important markets located along
the Missouri river were so high in comparison with
those from other lumber-producing towns as to operate
to its serious prejudice and disadvantage. There was
no contention that the charges from Eau Claire were
excessive, considered separately, and the railway principally interested manifested a willingness to reduce
them, but insisted that it could not by such action establish charges relatively satisfactory to the people of
Eau Claire, as any reduction it might make would be,
and when experimentally attempted had been, immediately neutralized by corresponding reductions from
other points made by railways which did not reach Eau
Claire. In its decision the Commission said:

"As it seems to us, this town (Eau Claire) has been placed
at a manifest disadvantage. So far from enjoying equal opportunity with its rivals, it appears to have been overweighted
with a differential which has excluded it, to a great extent,
from the field of competition. A number of its establishments

have gone out of business, its industrial development has been checked and its population seriously diminished. While neighboring towns have been prosperous, Eau Claire has not held its own."

And in ordering such a substantial reduction as in its opinion would render the charges from the competitive producing points relatively reasonable, the Commission added:

"Nor will any such consequences follow a reduction of the Eau Claire differential as would justify other carriers in lowering their rates at competing points for the purpose of preserving the correlation of rates. * * * Undoubtedly those roads have it in their power to continue the present disparity * *"

The rates from Eau Claire to the Missouri river points which the Commission had indicated were immediately promulgated by the defendant carrier, but the adjustment sought was as promptly nullified by reductions in the rates from the competing lumber towns that were served by railways which, as they did not reach Eau Claire, could not be said to discriminate unjustly against that place. Nor, though accepting the conclusions of fact reached by the Commission, does it appear clear that this action on the part of railways the volume of whose traffic was dependent upon their success in competing not merely with the railways serving Eau Claire, but, together with their auxiliaries, the lumber producers at other points, with a combination consisting of the producers of lumber at Eau Claire and the railways over which they shipped, deserved to be stigmatized as "inconsiderate and arbitrary." These railways had properly but two objects to attain,—first, fully to perform their *quasi*-public functions as carriers, and, second, to secure for their owners the reasonable return upon their investments tacitly agreed upon by the society whose agents they were. This society had, wisely or unwisely, declared that they should be operated independently of and in competition with other railways, and in separating thus sharply the interests of different railways, had made the refusal of traffic that would provide a reasonable revenue inconsistent with the objects named. The only questions to be asked in connection with the rates on lumber from the towns competing with Eau Claire, promulgated before or after the order of the Commission, was whether in comparison with other charges made by the same companies they were reasonable and just. If so, to make them higher in order that the lumber shipments of Eau Claire might be increased, would have been grossly unjust to the competing towns. Such difficulties are to be solved by a readjustment of the relations among railways and not by placing restrictions upon *independent* carriers.

It is perfectly clear that instances similar to the foregoing, borne frequently without complaint because they are regarded as inevitable, must continue to be numerous until some means is provided for treating as a unit all railways which participate in the performance of such closely related transportation services. Unjust discrimination among places will also continue as long as the traffic of certain localities is actively sought by rival railways competing in the only manner in which such competition has ever been made effective, by means of offers, secret or otherwise, to perform identical services for varying rates of compensation, while the business of other localities is thrown undivided to carriers, which are thus permitted to recoup the losses sustained in connection .with competitive business. Relatively fair rates at competitive points as compared with those charged at non-competitive points can be maintained only by the substantial elimination of the competitive element. This unquestionably involves agreement in regard to charges among the potentially rival carriers, and experience has shown that such agreements in order to be permanently effective must so far combine the interests of such carriers as to remove the temptation to violate them which is usually found in the temporary increase of revenue, or at least of tonnage, which can be gained by the secret acceptance of slightly lower rates than those agreed upon.

CHAPTER XX.

CHARGES FOR LONG AND SHORT HAULS.

One of the practices very frequently resulting from competition among railways which to the general public, always prone to assume that each service performed by a railway has its separate cost to the operating corporation and that charges should be proportional to such costs, seems least defensible is that of exacting a greater aggregate compensation for a shorter intermediate transportation service than for the movement of the same commodity in the same direction over a longer distance, including that for which the greater charge is made. This practice was quite common all over the country prior to the passage of the interstate-commerce law, by which it was made illegal in all cases in which both services are performed subject to "substantially similar circumstances and conditions" but has subsequently become much less frequent though it has not disappeared. It unquestionably constitutes a discrimination among localities, but, if the principles so far advanced in this series are sound, cannot be said to be unjust unless the disparity in charges fails to correspond with actual differences in the conditions governing the different services. This, though perhaps not yet completely understood by the general public, has become the commonly accepted view among students of transportation, though there remains some divergence of opinion as to what circumstances are adequate to justify the apparently preferential treatment of the longer distance traffic.

A lower charge for a particular service than for an intermediate one of the same kind is usually the result of conditions which make it appear impossible for the railway to obtain the longer distance traffic at rates which, if applied to all its business, would adequately or fairly remunerate its employes and owners. For purposes of illustration the case of a road carrying coal to a market at X, in which there is a demand for 30,000 tons per month at $4.50 per ton, may be supposed to be as described by the following statement:

Mines available.	Distance from X in miles.	Maximum capacity per month in tons.	Cost of production at mine per ton.	Rate to X per ton.	Cost of production at X per ton.
A 100		4,000	$3.00	$1.00	$4.00
B 130		5,000	2.80	1.25	4.05
C 150		6,000	2.75	1.40	4.15
D 175		7,000	2.70	1.50	4.20
E 200		8,000	3.25	1.25	4.50

It is essential to this illustration that the five mines shown be supposed to be all which can supply coal at X within the price per ton which will be paid for 30,000 tons, to be located on the main line of a single railway, and that other particulars are substantially as indicated in the table.

It is generally understood that the price of a particular commodity in any market varies inversely to the supply, and that if a certain quantity is called for at a given price a supply in excess of that quantity will reduce the price and one less than demanded will increase it. As none of the mines in question would be continuously operated unless the miners could realize the amount per ton indicated in the fourth column, it is evident that in the case supposed the railway must carry coal from E to X for $1.25 or less per ton or the latter

will not have the supply which it requires, and the price
will in consequence rise above $4.50.   It is true that the
railway might reduce the rates from the intermediate
mines to $1.25 or lower, but this could not have the
effect of increasing the traffic from those points and it
might reduce the aggregate earnings below the point
at which they would be reasonably remunerative.   Such
action would not benefit consumers at X, for the price
at that point would continue to be fixed by the cost of
that produced under the least advantageous circumstances,—viz, at E.   The amounts of the reductions, if
made, like the differences between the amounts in the
last column and the price at X, would become economic
rent, and would accrue not to the labor or capital
devoted to mining but as royalties to the owners of the
mines.   If therefore accepting traffic seeking shipment
from E to X at $1.25 per ton leaves the railway in as
good a financial condition as it would enjoy were it
rejected, i.e., if the revenue received from such shipments is sufficient to pay all expenses which would not
have been incurred had they not been carried, and if,
as has been supposed, it is all that can be collected without restricting shipments below 8000 tons per month,
the rate from E to X is not only justifiable but any
different rate would be unreasonable and unjust.

Another possibility might be considered in connection with the table.   Let it be assumed that the supply
of coal furnished by the mines A, B, C and D has
sufficed for X; that the rates shown in the fifth column
have been regularly collected, and that these, as well as
all of the rates collected by the railway for other services, have been absolutely and relatively reasonable

and just. The price of coal at X under such circumstances would have been $4.20 per ton. Now, if on account of an increase in population or for any other reason there is an augmentation of the demand for coal at X, the price will rise; let it be supposed that it rises to $4.50 per ton, and that the railway then commences to accept coal for shipment from E to X at $1.25. Then if the additional expense entailed by the movement of the new traffic is but $6000 per month, or 75 cents per ton, the railway's net earnings will be increased $4000; and, as the railway cannot reasonably be permitted to increase its net earnings, which were assumed to be already sufficient, this must be offset by the reduction of rates on other traffic. Those who have followed the discussion in these articles will not need to be reminded that this result will usually be secured by the free action of commercial forces, to struggle against which the railways are practically powerless.

Under present conditions, as was intimated in the beginning of this article, the inability to secure as high rates as are secured on intermediate traffic from business received at the points from which lower charges are made is usually the result of competition in some of its forms. Thus the competition of steamship lines doing business from New York city and other Northern Atlantic seaports to New Orleans is of such controlling force that it appears to justify the railways connecting those cities in the acceptance of much lower rates than are fair and reasonable on intermediate traffic for which the water route is not available. The same form of competition is met with at Galveston, and its effects extend into Texas and limit the rates which can be

obtained for railway service to many of the inland
cities of that state.

The Interstate Commerce Commission has consistently held, since the first case involving the fourth
section of the interstate commerce law which came
before it, that the dissimilar circumstances and conditions necessary to justify higher rates for intermediate
services may result from the competition of railways
which are not subject to the laws of the United States,
and has quite recently authorized certain of the railways
of this country to make exceptions from the general
rule on account of the competition of the Canadian
Pacific Railway. The Commission also, in a very early
case, expressed its opinion that under rare and peculiar
circumstances such substantial dissimilarity may result
from the competition of railways subject to the
law, and has, under the proviso of the fourth section,
considered applications for relief from the general rule
of that section based upon such grounds.

There appears to be no difficulty in justifying the
practice in question in the same manner as in the case
illustrated in the statement as long as the disparity in
rates merely measures with accuracy substantial differences in the conditions governing each shipment. It
is quite evident, however, that the lower charges for
transportation services which are actually greater do
unnecessarily favor particular localities, and that they
may offset natural advantages so far as to result in an
undesirable adjustment of productive industry. Yet
when these charges are justified by railway competition
it is society, which through the exercise of its legislative
power has imposed the maintenance of competition

upon reluctant railways, that is at fault and not the carriers. If the results appear undesirable, the circumstances which justify them can be readily removed by relieving the railway system from the burden of competing for traffic.

CHAPTER XXI.

UNJUST DISCRIMINATION AMONG COMMODITIES.

It is obvious that every manufacturer is interested
in the rates of freight not only on the raw materials
which he purchases and the commodities which he produces, but also in those exacted for moving the materials and products of his competitors. As manufacturers who compete in common markets are quite frequently located at very widely separated points it is apparent that the amounts charged for services quite different from those performed in his own behalf are very
often of the greatest importance to a particular manufacturer. One phase of this interdependence of rates
appears in the interest which a manufacturer, doing
business at a point located somewhere between the
region from which raw materials are obtained and the
communities in which the finished products made from
them are consumed, has in the charges for moving raw
materials similar to those he uses over the routes which
are regularly traversed by the commodities which he
manufactures. If the rates on the latter are reasonable
relatively to the charges exacted for carrying the same
commodity from the localities in which his competitors
do business to the common market, it is evident that the
interest is not in the aggregate amounts actually paid,
but in the relation which the charges on raw materials
bear to those on the finished product. An illustration
may be useful. A very large portion of the wheat produced in the Northwest is gathered at the mills of Minneapolis, and after being made into flour is shipped east-

ward to feed residents of the Eastern states and of Europe. The identical routes traversed by this flour are traversed also by wheat which is ground into flour much nearer the points of consumption than Minneapolis. It takes four and one-half bushels of wheat weighing, approximately, 270 pounds to make 196 pounds of flour, which with the barrel in which it is usually placed is accepted by the railways at an arbitrarily estimated weight of 200 pounds. Now if it be assumed that the advantage in cost of milling enjoyed by Minneapolis amounts to ten cents per barrel, and that the rate on flour from Minneapolis to a point on the Atlantic seaboard is seventy-five cents per barrel, it is evident that whenever the rate on wheat from Minneapolis to the same point falls below twenty-four cents per 100 pounds it becomes more profitable to mill at the Atlantic seaboard point than at Minneapolis. If the rate on wheat is twenty cents per 100 pounds the advantage at the seaboard will amount to eleven cents per barrel, and at fifteen cents it will be twenty-four and one-half cents. Probably even less than the smaller of these advantages, if continued throughout an extended period, would transfer the milling business of the Northwest, except in so far as it is conducted to furnish flour for local use, to the Atlantic seaboard.

The extensive traffic in dressed meats received by the railways which connect the various cities situated on the banks of the Missouri river, as well as St. Louis and Chicago, with the centers of population in the East furnishes another illustration of the same character. In spite of the magnitude of the interests represented it is unquestionable that if the present adjustment of rates was altered so as to be sufficiently unfavorable to shipments of meats the traffic in live cattle and hogs, which has by no means been discontinued, would be rapidly augmented, and in time the slaughtering and packing industries removed to localities much nearer the consumers.

Similarly rates on many commodities have an important relation to those applied to others which can be substituted. Thus anthracite coal, though preferred for many purposes over bituminous coal, may be entirely excluded from a particular market by an adjustment of charges which is relatively sufficiently favorable to the latter. Many other instances of both kinds will readily occur to the reader.

Discussion of relative rates appears often to be based upon an assumed obligation of the carriers to favor certain locations for particular industries, or in other cases to neutralize natural advantages so as to establish among those engaged in production at different points, an artificial equality in the competition of a common market. Neither of these assumptions has a reasonable basis. Society requires the production of commodities at the lowest practicable cost, not their production at a particular point or at a number of points. The competition to be favored is a natural competition which will discover and take advantage of the localities and methods best adapted for each form of production. If one competitor is artificially favored in order to create a fictitious equality the social cost of the total supply of the commodity he produces is inevitably enhanced. The force of commercial competition will lead manufacturers to seek the locations most advantageous from an economic standpoint if railway rates are adjusted independently of any desire to control or affect their location, and with a purpose merely to secure the most complete utilization of transportation agencies and the movement of all traffic that can recompense adequately the expenditure of energy required for its carriage.

Though the results of unjust discriminations of the character just described can be much more readily detected than those of discriminations among less closely related commodities it is quite possible to conceive an adjustment of charges which would impose upon one or more commodities an unjust share of the aggregate cost of railway transportation, thus giving all other commodities an unfair advantage. Thus as competition among railways connecting the same points, unquestionably, causes lower rates to be applied to traffic shipped between such points, and as the articles composing the bulk of such traffic are very often peculiar thereto, and do not traverse the same lines between local stations, there is a manifest discrimination that is unfavorable to the articles which make up the traffic to and from the latter points. It is also possible that the present distribution of the total expense of transportation bears with undue severity upon some of the great classes of commodities. Manufactured products may be unjustly favored at the expense of agricultural products, or *vice versa*. Animals and animal products may pay less than their share, and the balance may be collected from cereals, or from cotton, or from the local traffic in the products of truck farms destined to feed great cities. Whether the present adjustment is the best possible could be determined, if at all, only after the com-

pletest and most comprehensive investigation, but it
may be regarded as reasonably certain that whatever
evils of the character indicated now exist are the consequences of the lack of unity in the railway system.
Separately owned and independently operated railways
cannot perform in the highest possible manner the functions of a transportation system, because, among other
reasons, it is impracticable to apply to them on any
broad and comprehensive plan any scheme of relatively
reasonable charges. A railway in New England cannot properly be said to discriminate against the cotton
producers of Texas and Arkansas, though the entire
country might gain, in a manner which would favorably
affect the residents and railway owners of New England
as well as the planters of the Southwest, by the adoption
of a legal system by which the advantages of the more
compact traffic of one section might be extended over
the lines of a consolidated railway system serving the
whole country.

CHAPTER XXII.

THE PRESENT ADJUSTMENT OF RATES.

Though it will not be claimed that the relations now existing among the charges for railway services are, in all cases, those which are most desirable a spirit of wise conservatism will insist upon full consideration before accepting any plan involving radical modifications. The body of railway charges has not developed hastily nor are many of its inter-relations accidental. The extremely large number of officials having practically independent rate-making authority has given it an elasticity that though almost too free from reasonable limitations, when considered from some standpoints, has made it capable of yielding readily to new conditions, and to respond promptly to the growing demands upon transportation facilities of increasing commerce and multiplying territorial exchanges. The process is never complete, though it has dealt for three-quarters of a century with the rates of many railways, and has not failed to act upon those of the newest road in existence.

Classification of freight is now in a large sense the basis of the adjustment of charges for moving commodities, but no classification is so inviolable as to constitute a serious obstacle to necessary readjustments. Very early in the history of railways the increasing multiplicity of the different articles shipped made it inconvenient to establish separate rates for each commodity, and those of similar value, bulk, weight, etc., were grouped in classes for rate-making purposes. The development of classifications for this purpose was general and rapid, though without uniformity. At the close of the year 1886 nearly every railway had a freight classification of its own which it applied to strictly local traffic, and many roads were parties to several joint classifications applicable to traffic between terminals or traversing two or more connecting lines. The requirements of the Interstate Commerce law, and particularly of its long and short haul clause, made it almost wholly impracticable to conduct local and through business in accordance with its provisions under separate and frequently conflicting classifications, and as competition had already made uniformity in classification among rival routes indispensable there was a strong movement toward complete uniformity. At the present time three great classifications, each prevailing within an extensive territory, together determine relations among charges on the greater portion of the railway traffic of the country. Each of these great classifications is in charge of a committee composed of representatives of the different railways interested, and every alteration or exception must have its approval before rates thereunder are promulgated. The articles excepted from these classifications are usually those of relatively low value, which move in very large quantities, but even with regard to these commodities certain relations established by custom are rarely even temporarily abrogated. Thus throughout the entire North and West wheat and flour move at the same rates per hundred pounds.

When a new line is opened, and it becomes necessary to promulgate rates for the different services which it will have to perform, the freight classification applying to traffic within the territory in which it is located is made the basis of the new rates, and if there is no rival route available for the traffic which is sought, the rates of which must be considered as controlling those of the new route, the rates applied to each of the several classes will naturally be made progressive, the average per ton per mile declining gradually as the distance increases, and the cost of terminals is consequently distributed over a longer carriage. Seldom, however, does this simple adjustment of rates persist during any considerable period. Opportunities to increase traffic by lowering rates from or to particular points are presenting to the rate-making official by interested shippers, and if the former is convinced that the additional revenue received will exceed the extra expenses incurred on account of the new increment of traffic the concessions requested are promptly and gladly granted.

In another case it may appear that the traffic received at a particular station is decreasing, and the railway officials, always quick to perceive a change of this character, and to seek its cause, may find that the principal product upon which the community depends in its exchanges with other communities has been marketed in competition with the product of a distant region which has gained an advantage sufficient to give it practical control of the common market by means of cheaper transportation thereto. If, meeting with such a condition, the railway officials are unwilling to lose the traffic of the community so affected the only course open to them is to reduce their charges sufficiently to restore the former equilibrium, not for the purpose of controlling conditions in a particular market, as might too hastily be assumed, but to prevent serious depletion of the railway's revenue, and in order that it may not fail to move all the traffic that is seeking shipment. Obviously such reductions should not go beyond the point at which it is more profitable for the railway to carry the traffic affected than to leave it.

In ordinary cases successive modifications of this character, giving increased complexity to the schedule of rates, finally reach the point at which the railway receives and transports, at any particular time, a volume of traffic which approximates very closely the total amount of transportation which is socially desirable in the region which it serves, and receives therefor an aggregate revenue that constitutes a sufficient and reasonable remuneration for the energy employed.

At this point it may be assumed that an event occurs which has been too characteristic of the development of the railway system. There being no effective restraint on the construction of new railway lines, however adequately those in existence are serving the regions which they traverse, speculators are permitted as nearly as possible to parallel the line, and though topographical conditions do not, usually, permit absolute parallelism, and consequently competition at every point is impossible, there is an immediate struggle for traffic at meeting points. Reductions by the new line must be met by its competitor or traffic will be diverted, and in this way lower charges for longer than for intermediate shorter services arise as well as other differences which must operate unfavorably to the towns served by the old line only. Similar readjustments may be caused by the competition of circuitous routes or of water lines.

Almost innumerable causes similar to those described

have acted upon the relations among rates for services, many of which though apparently not connected have in reality the closest interdependence, and as their result have produced the present adjustment of charges. The latter is far from perfect, and may operate unjustly upon the interests of particular classes of traffic, communities, and individuals, but it is a part of a commercial system which is at once the most extensive and the most satisfactory that has been anywhere developed. Changes should unquestionably be made, not merely to accommodate the system to changing conditions, but more satisfactorily to meet the necessities of those now existent. Yet the attempt to alter and modify should be accompanied by a desire to conserve the commercial fabric which is based on transportation, and any change made should be preceded by the most complete and thorough study of all the interests which may be however remotely affected.

CHAPTER XXIII.

CONSOLIDATION.

In the preceding chapters it has been shown that competition among railway carriers results in higher average charges, without, however, gaining greater returns for railway owners; and in unjust discriminations the responsibility for which is popularly attributed to railway managers who are actually powerless to prevent them. It would, indeed, have been possible to go much further, and to demonstrate that it is very largely in consequence of the costly burden of unnecessary and socially undesirable competition among railways that, as stated in the latest annual report of the statistician to the Interstate Commerce Commission, dividends are paid upon less than thirty per cent. of the total outstanding railway stock and interest upon but seventeen per cent. of income bonds, while even of bonds secured by mortgages thirteen and one-half per cent. are in default. As these facts are necessarily most perceptible to railway owners and managers, it is by no means surprising that as soon as the railway facilities of the United States reached a stage of development which permitted competition on any considerable scale, efforts were made to mitigate its consequences and to secure the benefits of combination. These efforts have assumed many forms, but have produced results the most satisfactory, both to railway owners and to the general public, when they have aimed at the actual consolidation of lines owned by separate corporations. The process of consolidation has proceeded along two fairly distinct lines. The first, chron-

ologically, is the formation of such lines as those operated by the New York Central and Hudson River
Railroad, the Pennsylvania companies, and many others,
by the union of short connecting lines. The main line
of the former road was constructed and for a time operated, by eleven companies, ten of which forming the
line from Albany to New York, were consolidated as the
New York Central Railroad in 1853; the line from New
York to Albany, which had been independently operated
for eighteen years, being added in 1869. The addition
in 1873 of the New York and Harlem Railroad to the
properties operated by the same company is an illustration of the second phase of consolidation—that of parallel lines. Much of the latter has taken the form of
leases, the lessor companies sometimes continuing their
operating organizations. In other cases the practical
merging of parallel railways in a single organization
has been accomplished by the purchase of controlling
interests by the same individual or group of individuals,
and does not find expression in the form of their corporate organizations. The following table shows the
progress of consolidation as far as it can be traced statistically, but does not include those practical consolidations which have not affected the operating organizations. The data for 1892 and 1896 are from the reports
of the Statistician to the Interstate Commerce Commission and are substantially complete. Those for 1867
represent 46.61 per cent.; for 1872, 68.40 per cent.; for
1877, 87.32 per cent.; for 1882, 89.44 per cent., and for
1887, 87.81 per cent. of the entire railway mileage in
operation. It is probable that the inclusion of all roads,
had it been practicable, would have increased the pro-

portions in the classes embracing the shorter lines. In other words, the table does not show the full relative increase of mileage operated by the more important corporations:

Items.	Mileage over 1000.	Mileage from 600 to 1000.	Mileage from 400 to 600.	Mileage from 250 to 400.	Mileage under 250.	Total.
1867.						
Number of roads......................	1	3	7	11	72	94
Aggregate mileage in class......	1,152	2,252	3,440	3,189	7,183	17,216
Per cent. of total mileage...	6.69	13.08	19.98	18 52	41.73	100.00
1872.						
Number of roads......................	6	12	7	21	226	272
Aggregate mileage in class......	6,910	9,050	3,523	6,331	17,460	43,274
Per cent. of total mileage...	15.97	20.91	8.14	14.63	40 35	100.00
1877.						
Number of roads......................	11	12	17	34	362	436
Aggregate mileage in class......	13,648	8,807	8,154	10,700	26,388	67,697
Per cent. of total mileage...	20.16	13.01	12.04	15.81	38.98	100.00
1882.						
Number of roads......................	19	14	20	48	400	501
Aggregate mileage in class......	35,950	11,179	9,807	15,720	24,814	97,470
Per cent. of total mileage...	36.88	11 47	10.06	16.13	25.46	100.00
1887.						
Number of roads......................	28	19	27	53	434	561
Aggregate mileage in class......	55,447	14,671	13,860	16,694	26,373	127,045
Per cent. of total mileage...	43.64	11.55	10.91	13.14	20.76	100.00
1892.						
Number of roads......................	43	24	24	40	871	1,002
Aggregate mileage in class......	99,232	18,052	12,307	12,796	29,115	171,502
Per cent. of total mileage...	57 86	10.53	7.17	7.46	16 98	100 00
1896.						
Number of roads......................	44	22	24	44	977	1,111
Aggregate mileage in class......	103,346	17,450	12,158	14,226	34,498	181,678
Per cent. of total mileage...	56.89	9.60	6.69	7.83	18.99	100.00

By means of these consolidations the public has gained better service than would have been possible had it remained necessary for each shipment over an average distance to traverse several independent lines, and has also been accorded such service at a much lower aggregate cost than would have been required had so many separate operating organizations been maintained.

Besides the process of corporate consolidation, there

has gone on another evolutionary change which has also tended toward the practical unification of the railway system. Among the characteristics of this change are the arrangements by which travelers having to traverse the lines of several independent railways have been enabled usually to purchase tickets and check baggage from starting-point to destination and frequently to make the entire journey without leaving the train, those for the interchange of freight cars which permit shipments to traverse independent lines without transfers from car to car, and those for joint classifications, through rates, and bills of lading. That consolidation, though perhaps not always in the legal sense, is a natural and necessary incident of railway development is indicated by the fact that the process in one form or another has gone on in spite of and scarcely hindered by the numerous artificial obstacles that have had to be overcome. Inspired by public sentiment, which has only lately taken cognizance of the fact that competition in the ordinary sense is both undesirable and impracticable among railways, provisions intended to restrict consolidations have been incorporated in state constitutions, in acts of state legislatures, and in railway charters. The Federal Congress has prohibited agreements for the division of traffic or earnings, and possibly, even agreements to make and maintain reasonable rates. Cities have strenuously opposed arrangements which would prevent the unloading and transfer within their limits of freight passing through them, and railways have been constructed with gauges differing from those of their connections in order that cars should not pass from one to the other. Yet through cars and shipments

have become the general rule, and the standard gauge
has been substituted in nearly every instance where
either narrow or broad gauges were originally constructed.   When an industrial tendency strong enough
to override laws enacted for its control is discovered, it
is reasonable to conclude that it serves some beneficent
purpose and wise legislators will aim to take advantage
of it rather than to place obstacles in its path.   In the
case of railway consolidation the presumption of benefi-
cence is supported by experience and by the judgment
of those most acquainted with the facts concerning the
transportation industry.

CHAPTER XXIV.

POOLING PRIOR TO 1887.

The practice, popularly, though somewhat carelessly and incorrectly termed pooling, is resorted to by railways which compete for traffic between the same points in order to eliminate from the cost of operation the wasteful expenditures incident to the struggle for traffic and incidentally to obviate the necessity of making rates apparently too favorable to the traffic affected by the competition. It is an expedient intended to secure to railway owners and patrons some of the benefits of consolidation when the complete merging of rival interests is not desired or is for any reason impracticable.

Pooling contracts may be defined as those which provide for the division between two or more railways of traffic which might go by either, or all or a portion of the earnings therefrom, in proportions set forth in the contract or determined in accordance with its terms. Contracts for the division of revenue, whether gross or net, are termed "money pools" and had existed in England for many years before being introduced in this country. "Tonnage pools" aim to secure the physical division of common business, diverting traffic from lines in excess to those which have received less than their agreed shares of the aggregate tonnage.

Though the pools earliest established in this country were among the New England railways, they were comparatively unimportant, and the system first attained considerable development in the region traversed by the so-called "granger" roads. One of the most in-

teresting, on account of the exceptionally long period of
its uninterrupted existence and the simplicity of its
machinery, included freight and passenger traffic carried between Chicago and Omaha, and continued from
1870 until superseded by a new organization in 1882.
For seventeen years prior to the passage of the Interstate Commerce law there was but one period, and that
of less than twelve months' duration, in which the traffic
between these points was not subject to a pooling arrangement. The principal lines engaged in carrying
anthracite coal to the Atlantic seaboard arranged a pool
which went into operation on December 1, 1872, continuing until August, 1876. A pooling arrangement
embracing the four roads connecting Atlanta, Ga., with
the seaboard was formed in December, 1873; a money
pool applying to both passenger and freight traffic between Chicago or Milwaukee and St. Paul took effect
on September 1, 1874; the so-called "cattle eveners"
pool and the South Western Railway Association, a
pooling organization, were organized during 1875; the
Southern Railway and Steamship Association pool during 1876; and the Trunk Line Association pool during
1877. During 1878 it was authoritatively stated that
the Illinois Central Railroad participated in more than
twenty pools in the two states of Illinois and Iowa, and
that the Chicago and Alton Railway was a party to
twelve such arrangements.

Agreements for the division of competitive traffic or
the earnings therefrom constituted a most interesting,
conspicuous and characteristic feature of American railway administration at the time of the passage of the Interstate Commerce law. Though that law expressly

forbade all such arrangements, the manner in which the prohibitory clause was forced into the measure and the much greater frequency of acknowledgments of the necessity of pooling and of its beneficial results than of objections thereto in the testimony taken during the preliminary investigation of the Committee on Interstate Commerce of the United States Senate justifies the statement that the familiarity of the public with pooling arrangements had not resulted in any preponderance of public sentiment in favor of their prohibition.

Indeed, whatever public condemnation the pooling system received aside from that inspired by the irresponsible utterances of demagogues, who found attacks upon railway corporations just as their prototypes a few decades earlier had found the popular enthusiasm for railway construction, an easy and convenient means of attaining office, was due rather to the fact that those arrangements were never permanent, and in consequence never wholly eradicated the evils they should have corrected.   Though after nearly a decade spent in the study of the social aspects of railroad transportation from the standpoint of a public official, Dr. Joseph Nimmo stated in the annual report of the Bureau of Statistics of the United States Treasury Department for 1879 that railway pooling had come to be favored by the general public because it had proved to be "the means of arresting discriminations"; and the Iowa Railroad Commission in its report for 1878 expressed the same idea by declaring that it considered "the pool as the only agency that can compel the through traffic to bear, as it should, its proportion of the interest on the cost and the expenses of maintaining and operating the roads"; Mr. Albert Fink, the originator, organizer and official head of the most complete pooling association ever established, was at almost the same time complaining of their lack of permanence and stability and consequent inadequacy, and urging the necessity of legislation to give them legal sanction and effect.

All railway pools in the United States have been extra-legal arrangements, dependent for their execution upon the good faith of the parties, upon the violation of which none of them would venture to appeal to the courts for redress. So lacking were these arrangements in the necessary cohesive qualities that each railway considered their abrogation an inevitable incident, pending which constant vigilance was necessary in order that the day of dissolution should not find it an unready or tardy contestant in the struggle for traffic. The period during which a pooling contract was in operation was consequently one of armed neutrality, and, as in many cases between nations, that relation was regularly disturbed by instances of depredations by irresponsible members of the rival forces. As the apportionment of business in any pool which should follow a period of warfare would probably be based upon the proportions offered (if a tonnage pool) and carried (if a money pool) prior to the disruption of such an agreement, there was a strong incentive to take advantage of every opportunity to gain traffic by its violation which promised immunity from detection. Thus there was never an entire abandonment of the baneful practices of competition, there were always discriminations in favor of competitive traffic, and there were frequent periods during which all the evils of unjust discrimination operated to

their fullest extent.   Nevertheless, as indicated in the
quotation from the Iowa Railroad Commission, the
evils of excessive competition were in some degree mitigated, and the pooling arrangements, unstable and unsatisfactory as they too frequently were, indicated a
means of securing in some measure that substantial
identity among the interests of the carrying corporations which is a prerequisite to the lowest and most
equitably adjusted rates.

CHAPTER XXV.

POOLING UNDER FEDERAL SUPERVISION.

Immediately upon the passage of the Interstate Commerce law all pooling contracts were discontinued, and there is evidence that nearly all railways sought in good faith to observe its provisions. Railway associations were formed which announced as their objects the maintenance of reasonable rates and the enforcement of the regulative provision of the new law. The co-operation of the weaker lines was in many instances purchased by permission to charge slightly lower rates than those collected by their stronger rivals. Subsequently other efforts were made to effect the satisfactory division of traffic without its actual transfer from one line to another after consignment, and without resort to the methods technically characteristic of tonnage pools; but the practical failure of these measures is now generally recognized, and the patrons as well as the owners and managers of railway properties are now urging a modification of the Interstate Commerce law that will permit agreements for the apportionment of traffic; operations thereunder to be conducted under the strict supervision of Federal authorities. This change has been recommended by several annual conventions of national and state railway commissioners, by the National Board of Trade, by a conference of representatives of boards of trade and other commercial organizations of the principal cities of this country, and has received the approval of individual members of the Interstate Commerce Commission and of the author of the anti-pooling section of the present law. A bill embodying it and including several other very desirable amendments to the Interstate Commerce law, which had been strongly urged by the Commission, passed the House of Representatives during the last session of the Fifty-third Congress, and would unquestionably have received the support of a large majority of the Senate had not the rules of that body and the early approach of the end of the session, combined with the obstructive tactics of a minority, numerically insignificant, prevented its friends from securing a vote upon its passage.

In its eleventh annual report the Interstate Commerce Commission expressed its opinion that:

"It is only by destroying competition that the inducement to deviate from the published rate is wholly removed, and it is only to the extent that competition is actually destroyed that beneficial results can be expected,"

and in the last chapter it was intimated that the weakness of the pooling system as formerly conducted arose from the instability and temporary character of the pooling agreements. Attention should be directed to the essential difference in this particular between pooling as practiced prior to 1887 and the arrangements that will be permitted, subject to effective Federal supervision, should the Patterson or Foraker bill, or a similar measure be adopted by Congress. Indeed, whatever provision for pooling may be finally adopted, it is certain to be in a large degree free from the objections cited. The contracts permitted will have the express sanction of a Federal statute, and any railway corporation that may be injured by the failure of another to observe the terms of a pooling agreement to which both are parties may invoke judicial aid in securing the particular kind of redress that is found to be adequate and suitable. Such agreements will naturally provide for a definite period of operation, with, possibly, continuance thereafter subject to due notice of the intention of any party to withdraw. The possibility of unjust personal discriminations will, it may reasonably be hoped, be minimized by the discontinuance of separate soliciting for traffic, and the substitution of joint for independent ticket and freight agencies. Whenever the temporarily divergent interests of separate bodies of stock and bond-holders can be sufficiently subordinated to the general interest of all the carriers in the satisfactory adjustment of the railway system to the ends for which it exists, the latter will be found to constitute a powerful agency for the elimination of unjust discriminations, including those among competing localities and communities. When the exact proportion of competitive traffic which will fall to a particular route becomes as certain as that it will receive all of the non-competitive traffic, both will be treated with equity, for there will be no reason for favoring cities served by more than one railway. The selfish interests of carriers will then make powerfully for justice, while such regulative instrumentalities as may be established by the public will have the advantage of dealing with a railway system that has become unified and homogeneous.

In addition, the Federal supervision of the operations under pooling arrangements provided for in each of the measures which have recently been advocated in Congress is adequate and complete. In all such measures the supervisory functions have, very wisely, been delegated to the Interstate Commerce Commission, with which every contract for the division of traffic or earnings must be filed before it may become effective. The Commission is authorized and directed to disapprove any such contract when, in its opinion, it will, if permitted to go into effect, operate injuriously to the public by resulting in unreasonable rates, unjust discriminations, inferior service, or otherwise. The Commission is directed also to observe the working of each pooling arrangement and whenever facts appear which if apprehended would have warranted the disapproval of the contract in the first instance, is authorized to issue an order requiring the rates to be changed, the unjust discriminations to be stopped, the facilities to be improved, the improper practices to be corrected, or, in its discretion, requiring the entire discontinuance of the contract itself. Appeals to the Federal courts from orders of the Commission disapproving or annulling such contracts are allowed, but provision is made for their determination without delay, and while they are pending the operation of the contract is suspended. The recital of these provisions seems to be ample evidence that if pooling can be permitted at all, if it is desirable on any grounds, the privilege is likely, when granted, to be surrounded by sufficient safeguards. The frequently expressed willingness of railway owners and officials to accept the desired amendment on these terms indicates that they do not desire or expect to impose upon the public unjust or unreasonable charges for transportation services.

CHAPTER XXVI.

POOLING, CONSOLIDATION, OR UNJUST DISCRIMINATION.

The lesson most clearly taught by the history of railway transportation in the United States during the period subsequent to the passage of the Interstate Commerce law is the utter impracticability of preventing unjust discriminations in charges for railway services by any method that does not effectually limit competition, and that no such limitation is possible while rates for similar services are independently made by the officers of separate corporations.   Experience during the same period has also shown that the rates agreed upon will not be consistently maintained when that course results in serious financial loss.   Conflicting interests must be merged or reconciled, or unjust discriminations will continue to interfere injuriously with the conduct of industry.   In spite of the requirements of the Interstate Commerce law, the practices recently resorted to in the stress of competition have caused the current year to be described by one railway president as "a year of probably the greatest demoralization of rates that has ever been known," while another has written in the latest annual report to the stockholders of his company:

"The evil of rate-cutting seems to have passed from the acute to the chronic stage, and ordinary remedies are no longer effective."

The remedies possible have already been indicated, but it remains to consider which is now more expedient. Competition may be checked by general consolidation, and when the salutary results already secured through the process of unification are considered the desirability of its continuance seems proven. To admit that complete ultimate unification of the railway system may be desirable is, however, very different from agreeing that a natural process apparently leading to that result should be artificially stimulated. The question involves not merely the economic organization of transportation or of industry, but is also one of political adjustment. Nothing is plainer than the historical teaching that violent changes in political organization are seriously detrimental even when not actually destructive. The corporation owning railway property worth ten billions of dollars receiving twelve thousand millions of dollars in annual earnings, and having upon its pay-rolls eight hundred thousand voters, might be a creature of and nominally. subordinate to the state, or it might be the state itself. In the former case there would be thrown upon the judicial and other regulative authorities a burden of responsibility which they should not be forced to assume suddenly or otherwise than as the result of a steady growth, along with which such institutions would gradually develop capacity adequate to the new tasks. Consolidation under government ownership would in the same way devolve upon the public administrative agencies extensive duties for which they have not had the necessary preliminary training. Public administration in the United States is seriously weak, not because of the incapacity of their citizens, but because the functions of the several governments have been so restricted that administrative ability has sought and found its highest rewards in private enterprises. Whatever may be the final verdict in regard to government ownership of railways, there can be no controversy in regard to the wisdom of postponing it until it has become practicable to secure reasonably honest and business-like management of the municipal affairs of American cities.

Consolidation, then, as a natural process, is neither to be feared nor hindered, though, if unduly stimulated, it may develop dangers of a serious character. It is unduly stimulated when, by restricting or withdrawing the privilege of making contracts among themselves, it is made the only means of harmonizing the interests of railway corporations. The last decade has furnished abundant evidence of the truth of this assertion, both in the number of mergers of corporate identity and of less open attempts to secure the same results by purchases of controlling interests in formerly independent railways by single individuals or compact groups of individuals.

The statement of the form in which the privilege of apportioning traffic is proposed to be restored and the restrictions with which it is to be surrounded indicates that no violent or dangerous change is contemplated. The urgent need of provision for such agreements and the harmlessness of pooling were well expressed by the present chairman of the Interstate Commerce Commission in the paper quoted in the fourteenth article. He said:

"I am forced to the conclusion that the prohibition of pooling, which remains imbedded in the present statute, is irreconcilably at variance with its other provisions. To my mind the legislation which decrees that all rates shall be just and reasonable and declares unlawful every discrimination between individuals or localities, is plainly inconsistent with competitive charges. I regard the existing law as presenting this singular anomaly that it seeks to enforce competition by the mandate

of the statute, and at the same time to punish as criminal misde-
meanors the acts and inducements by which competition is
ordinarily effected."

And in another portion of the same article:

"It is entirely plain to me, therefore, that co-operative methods, the general discontinuance of competition *in rates* between
rival railroads would tend strongly to remove the inequalities
which now exist, and prove a positive and substantial advantage to the great majority of producers and consumers. And
I firmly believe that while there is a popular objection to railroad pooling, founded largely upon ignorance of its purpose
and misconception of its effects, the principal opposition to
legalized co-operation, the opposition which has thus far pre-
vailed, comes from the favored few who are reaping unearned
profits by the discriminating practices which they virtually
compel, and of which they are the sole beneficiaries."

On account of the anomaly in the Interstate Commerce law alluded to in the foregoing extract, Federal
railway regulation has so far proved of little utility. So
long as it remains in the statute unjust discrimination
will continue and the process of railway consolidation
will be unnaturally, perhaps harmfully, stimulated.

CHAPTER XXVII.

ASSOCIATIONS.

Though the title of this article might be applied with propriety to many organizations which have been formed to aid in the performance of the special functions of the different classes of labor applied to railway transportation, it is necessary to limit the present discussion to that group of associations which is distinguished by the common object of securing agreement among rival lines in regard to charges for the services each can perform and the continual observance of the schedule adopted. The subject of pooling having been already treated, the present article will be further limited to those associations during the period since the apportionment of traffic or earnings was made illegal by the Interstate Commerce law, and to the efforts which have been made to discover an effective substitute for the prohibited practice.

Many of the associations which had formerly exercised supervision over pooling arrangements were continued after the division of traffic had been abandoned, in obedience to the statute, for the avowed purpose of securing harmonious action in regard to rates on competitive business. The method of securing this result ordinarily adopted consists of frequent conferences among rate-making officials or other representatives of the railways interested, the submission of proposed rates to such conferences and their promulgation by joint authority if adopted. The rules of many associations require unanimous agreement in regard to changes in rates or regulations, and provide for the arbitration of differences that cannot otherwise be adjusted amicably. Provision is quite generally made for the collection of more or less complete statistics concerning the movement of competitive business, and the duties of the principal executive officer frequently include the investigation of suspected instances of violation of the association agreement by rate cutting or the manipulation of charges in such a way as to amount to a deviation from the published schedules.

In order to secure the permanent adherence of the lines supposed to be most strongly tempted to violate agreements in regard to rates, the railroads regarded as suffering particular disadvantages in competition for traffic have sometimes been permitted to charge lower rates than those exacted by their more fortunately situated rivals, it being expected that this concession would secure to the roads allowed to name the lower rates sufficient proportions of the aggregate traffic to induce them to observe the rates agreed upon and thus prevent general demoralization. It may be remarked in passing that this is a curious development of the commonly accepted theory that the purpose of agreements apportioning traffic is to secure to each carrier that portion of the total business which it would receive at *equal* rates and to which it is therefore assumed to be entitled. The differential system, though it is unquestionably adopted for the same real purpose, that of restricting competition, aims to secure for the carriers certain proportions which are avowedly different from those which they would receive were the rates by all routes the same. In other cases the agreements have specified the proportions to be considered equitable. and have attempted to secure the distribution of traffic in such proportions by requiring the cessation of efforts to secure traffic as soon as the agreed amount for the particular period determined upon has been received.

Among the disappointments which have come to railway managers during the period characterized by the prohibition of pooling, none has been more serious than the almost utter failure of every attempt to secure consistent co-operation in rate making. Agreements framed under apparently the most favorable auspices and assented to with the utmost solemnity have proved practically useless. Mutual distrust founded on jealousies of long standing and augmented by rumors, as frequently unfounded as otherwise, industriously circulated by interested shippers, has with persistent regularity turned harmony into demoralization, and out of the beneficent stability of industrial conditions due to the maintenance of rates brought the evils of rate-cutting and discrimination. To those who are familiar with the history of transportation during the last decade a list of the railway associations formed from time to time brings to mind a consecutive list of failures unredeemed by a single instance of substantial success.

In spite of these successive disappointments, those having charge of railway properties, seeing no other means by which they might hope to preserve the interests of railway investors from the losses of unrestricted competition and from the reproach of unjust discrimination, attempted again and again to organize new associations having greater elements of stability. One of the most elaborate of these is the Joint Traffic Association, which includes nearly all of the railways located in the territory north of the Potomac and Ohio rivers and between the Mississippi river and the Atlantic seaboard. The purposes of this association, as stated in the agreement for its organization, are:

"to aid in fulfilling the purposes of the Interstate Commerce Act, to co-operate with each other and adjacent transportation associations, to establish and maintain reasonable and just rates, fares, rules and regulations on state and interstate traffic, to prevent unjust discrimination and to secure the reduction and concentration of agencies and the introduction of economies in the conduct of the freight and passenger service."

The novel features of this association lent considerable interest to the experiment, which unquestionably had greater promise of success than most of its predecessors. The new organization had not fairly started, however, when the United States Supreme Court, reversing several decisions in the lower Federal Courts, declared that the anti-trust law is applicable to agreements among railways and that in prohibiting all contracts in restraint of trade Congress had forbidden agreements intended to secure reasonable charges, as well as those aiming to make possible the collection of unreasonable and excessive rates. This conclusion was announced in the decision in the Trans-Missouri Association case, and was dissented from by four of the justices. As there were material differences in the agreements upon which the associations were formed, the Joint Traffic Association has been continued. An action intended to secure its discontinuance was immediately begun by the Attorney-General of the United States and there can be no doubt that its activity and usefulness have been seriously impaired by the threat of unfavorable judicial action that has continually impended. The case now awaits decision in the Federal Supreme Court, and, though there have been changes in the Court which may modify its views, it would be useless to attempt to anticipate its conclusion. If it is unfavorable to the railways it will merely render the situation less satisfactory from a public standpoint as well as from that of the railways, and accentuate the necessity, already urgent, of a modification in the present law. If the association is permitted to continue there need be no congratulations among those who desire the prevention of unjust discrimination or the elimination of competitive wastefulness from railway administration. The experiment will still have against its chances of success the elements which have brought about the failure of all its predecessors since pooling became illegal, and though conducted in the territory where railway rates should be most readily maintained, is not unlikely to share the common fate. In any event, there are extensive regions with important industrial and railway interests in which, as is evident to those having but the slightest knowledge of current conditions, it would be impracticable successfully to maintain similar associations.

CHAPTER XXVIII.

TAXATION.

During the ten years covered by the reports of the statistician to the Interstate Commerce Commission an increase in the aggregate annual railway earnings from operation of 23.2 per cent. and one of 17.1 in the balance of such earnings over operating expenses, have been accompanied by an increase of 69.6 per cent. in the total annual payment toward the expenses of government required from railway corporations. The following statement shows for each year the earnings remaining after paying the cost of operation, the total payments for taxes and the relation of the latter to the former amount:

Year.	Net Earnings.	TAXES. Amount.	Per cent.
1888	$315,626,564	$25,435,229	8.06
1889	320,109,428	27,590,394	8.62
1890	359,783,661	31,207,469	8.67
1891	364,873,502	33,280,095	9.12
1892	390,409,347	34,053,495	8.72
1893	392,830,575	36,514,689	9.30
1894	341,947,475	38,125,274	11.15
1895	349,651,047	39,832,433	11.39
1896	377,180,332	39,970,791	10.60
1897	369,565,009	43,137,844	11.67

Aside from the large proportions of net earnings which have been regularly required from the railways the most noticeable feature presented by the foregoing statement is that the burden of taxation borne by the railways has increased with a regularity that has been uninterrupted by the fact that business depression, accompanied by diminished traffic and decreasing rates, has generally depleted the revenues of the carriers. This lack of definite relation between ability to pay and

taxation is very clearly illustrated in the following statement, which shows net earnings and taxes for each of
the groups adopted for the classification of railway statistics by the Interstate Commerce Commission. The
facts relate to the year ending with June 30, 1896, the
latest for which complete data are now available:

Group.	Net Earnings.	TAXES.	
		Amount.	Per cent.
I	$26,538,293	$3,282,819	12.37
II	97,200,773	7,997,873	8.23
III	50,306,072	6,362,005	12.65
IV	14,220,233	1,382,606	9.72
V	26,138,170	2,697,576	10.32
VI	91,641,910	8,868,810	9.68
VII	13,092,366	1,661,917	12.69
VIII	27,707,219	4,151,543	14.98
IX	9,871,324	1,176,188	11.92
X	20,463,972	2,389,454	11.68

It seems almost superfluous to attempt to add to the
indications of lack of uniformity presented by the foregoing statement, but it may be observed that if a tax
amounting to 12.37 per cent. of net earnings is proper
in Group I, that is made up of the six New England
States in which payments on account of railway capital
amount to 4.89 per cent. of its par value, a tax of 11.68
per cent. of the net earnings of the railways of Group X
(Washington, Oregon, California, Idaho, Nevada, Utah,
Arizona and part of New Mexico), in which payments
on account of capital constitute but 1.94 per cent. of its
par value, must be excessive. In the former group dividends were paid during 1896 on 79.14 per cent.: in the
latter on but 1.60 per cent. of the total stock outstanding. In the former interest was paid on all but 1.54
per cent. of the funded debt: in the latter 25.29 per cent.
was portionless. Taxes paid in Group I during 1896
amounted to 23.4 per cent. of the dividends during the

same year; in Group X the amount of taxes was 499.1 per cent. of that of dividends.

According to a recent report of the president of the Chicago and Alton Railroad, the gross earnings of that company have decreased from $7,687,226 in 1880 to $6,840,284 in 1896, and net earnings from $3,477,985 to $2,801,737; yet during the same years the taxes paid by the company have increased from $147,414, or 4.24 per cent. of net earnings, to $315,745, or 11.27 per cent. The same authority states that the total assessment of all property other than railroads in the State of Illinois was $892,380,972 in 1877 and $753,869,082 in 1895, showing an actual decrease in the valuation for purposes of taxation of about sixteen per cent., though it is a fact of general observation that there has been an actual and considerable increase in the real value of such property. During the same period the total railway mileage in the state was increased less than fifty per cent., and the net earnings from railway operation about forty per cent., but the assessment of railway property was more than doubled, being increased from $37,141,180, in 1877, to $79,231,164 in 1895, or 113.3 per cent.

The limits of this article will not permit a discussion of the causes which have resulted in levying such heavy taxes upon railway corporations, nor will it be practicable to consider the relative merits of the different systems of taxation which have been applied to and proposed in connection with railway properties. Some brief consideration of the general policy of railway taxation may, however, be serviceable. Taxes may be classified with regard to whether they are finally paid by the person from whom they are directly collected, and this is understood principally to be determined by the conditions governing the production of the thing taxed; if the latter is so restricted as to give an effective monopoly privilege to the producers they are supposed to exact at all times the particular prices which produce the greatest revenues above expenses and must consequently assume any tax that is levied upon them. If, on the other hand, the price of the article taxed is fixed by competition among producers, it will always so closely approximate the cost of producing the marginal increment of the supply that the amount of any tax must be added to the price. As railways are producers of place utilities, their ability to shift taxes must depend in a large measure upon whether the articles to which such utilities are added are sold at prices fixed by competition. Examination of the articles which make up the traffic of any particular railway will probably show that with regard to some of them it possesses an effective monopoly privilege, while the prices obtainable for others are fixed by competition of the fiercest character. If, in order to meet this competition, railways are regularly led to carry certain articles at rates which do not more than pay the cost of moving the trains in which they are carried and the other expenses actually and directly incurred in order to transport them, it may be that the entire proceeds of their business in connection with the monopolized portion of their traffic is necessarily expended in order to meet the reasonable demands of investors and to pay those expenses of operation which are incurred on account either of all traffic or of large classes of traffic, and that the average rate is reduced as rapidly as the cost of operation will permit. The relative importance of these classes of traffic might determine the result, but if it should be as suggested above, any tax collected from the railways would be by them transferred to their patrons.

There may be some doubt concerning the advisability of levying any tax at all upon railways, if it is admitted that it will be shifted to their patrons, but it cannot be discussed within the limits of the present article, though it may be remarked that such a tax, by increasing the cost of transportation, must limit the area within which commodities can profitably be marketed, and that, in consequence, any community which taxes the transportation agencies by which it is served more heavily and vigorously than those which serve competing regions are taxed, places itself at a disadvantage in common markets.

CHAPTER XXIX.

CONSTRUCTION.

Attention has been called in another chapter to the fact that the railway mileage annually constructed in the United States has varied widely, that of the year of greatest construction since 1880 being more than seven times that of 1897. These fluctuations seem to have had some regularity, the maximum construction having been attained soon after events which, like the high prices of food products during 1881, have resulted, for a time at least, in extraordinary prosperity, the decline having commenced somewhat before the culmination of those periods and continued until the usual reaction from extreme depression, has resulted in renewed industrial activity. This tendency to wave-like fluctuations apparently controlled by commercial conditions indicates the extreme sensitiveness of railway development to circumstances that affect the risk incurred by investors, and also that the consequences of this sensitiveness may in turn become causes which themselves operate adversely to industrial stability. A sudden stimulus to railway construction draws men from other occupations into the service of the firms and corporations engaged in building and in supplying material for constructing new lines or extending old ones, and thus rapidly augments the demand for labor throughout the country and in most industries. The same cause may affect immigration, and it is noticeable that the increases and decreases in the number of immigrants annually reaching the United States have been in some degree synchronous with the fluctuations in the same direction in railway construction. On the other hand, the slightest decrease in railway building throws men out of employment who thus cease to be consumers of the products of the labor of others and become competitors with them for employment in other occupations. It is quite obvious, therefore, that if by some means the increased railway mileage demanded by developing internal commerce could be supplied in more regular annual increments one serious source of industrial crises would be removed.

The desirability of limiting railway construction is also apparent from the standpoint of public interest in securing transportation at low and relatively reasonable rates. It is perfectly evident that society as a whole must pay for whatever transportation facilities it obtains, but the fact that it is the purchasers of transportation and not those who furnish the capital necessary for railway construction and equipment who must ultimately bear the expense of useless construction is quite frequently overlooked by the general public. Yet there is abundant evidence, not only that railway patrons must, in the long run, pay interest upon a sum equal to the aggregate capital actually invested in railway facilities, but that the rate of interest is increased by every circumstance that tends to enhance the risk attending such investments. The general failure to perceive the detrimental consequences of unnecessary construction is attributable to the fact that under a system of transportation in which competition among carriers for traffic between points at which several lines are available to shippers is encouraged, the burden of maintaining transportation facilities is so unfairly distributed that the communities served by two or more rival routes, finding themselves enjoying more favorable rates than those served by single lines and perceiving that the discriminations by which they profit are the result of competition, are led to believe that if there was no competition among railways seeking the same traffic, the relatively high rates charged at non-competitive points would be applied uniformly to all business. The communities discriminated against on account of their more limited facilities naturally regard as desirable the advantages enjoyed at the competitive points, and thus has arisen a strong incentive toward the duplication of facilities through the construction of lines substantially parallel to those already in existence. Much of the unprofitable railway construction has been due to this cause, though it is to be observed that the supposed remedy is applicable only at a few points, and tends to accentuate the disadvantages already felt by the communities which do not possess alternative routes.

Speculative construction has also entailed upon railway patrons the burden of paying interest on capital in the form of unnecessary railway facilities. When the railways serving a particular territory have abundant traffic and are earning satisfactory returns on the investments which they represent, it is quite evident that the construction of a new line may demoralize business so seriously as materially to impair, at least temporarily, the value and earning capacity of the lines already in existence. In this fact lies an opportunity which has frequently been turned to the advantage of adventurous speculators. A charter for a new line is unfortunately

quite easily procurable in most regions. Sometimes
securing such a charter is the only step taken, the fran-
chise itself being purchased by the lines with which the
new road would compete before the track has been laid,
the roadway graded or even accurately surveyed. Politicians of a certain sort have at times found it very
profitable to obtain such charters from complacent legislatures without at any time intending to make
any use of them except to dispose of them to
the highest bidders, who are usually those who
would suffer most were the project apparently in
hand actually executed. In other instances railways
have been actually constructed with no other object
than to demoralize rates until, choosing between two
evils, one of the older lines is compelled to purchase
the new one. In such cases the capital of the purchasing corporation is of course increased by the amount
paid, and though this may for awhile transform a profitable line into one scarcely able to keep out of insolvency, the new capital must be made eventually to pay
adequate dividends and interest, or, if the region served
is industrially stagnant or retrograding, the losses will
usually be made up from some other portion of the
country. The construction of such lines is nothing
more than a form of legalized blackmail, the losses of
which originally met by capitalists are almost invariably shifted from them to those who purchase railway
services.

During the last five years speculative and wasteful
construction in the United States has practically ceased
and many sections of the country have had opportunity
to develop up to the facilities created during the years

of over-construction. It is most important, however,
that, before the inevitable reaction from the recent commercial depression results in another period of too-
rapid railway building, the states which have not already
taken steps to provide suitable checks against the wasteful duplication of existing lines should do so. No railway can be constructed without the aid of government,
not only for the creation of the corporation but also in
order to secure the right of way by the exercise of the
power of eminent domain which is invoked on the
ground of the quasi-public purpose for which the
railway is to exist. Each community owes to itself
the duty of using its powers for these purposes carefully and intelligently, and to investors that of so limiting permission to construct new lines as to provide for
no greater aggregate investment than that upon which
it can afford and is willing to pay a reasonable return.
It is particularly necessary that means for preventing
the speculative construction of parallel lines should exist
whenever pooling arrangements are permitted, for the
existence of a pool considerably enlarges the field for
profitable operations of that character by offering opportunity to blackmail a compact group of railways with
unified interests of considerable extent in place of depre-